ZENTY

BY THE AUTHOR

Spring Comes First to the Willows

Zenty

ZENTY

HELEN MARIE PUNDT

Thomas Y. Crowell Company *New York*

To my parents, who never failed in devotion
to their children or to each other.

ZENTY

ONE

April spilled sunshine warmly over the upstairs porch where Aunt Doris had covered the floor with newspapers and set out the unfinished window boxes that one day soon would hold geraniums and ivy. A long table with benches attached had been pushed to the far end of the porch. There Zenty sat, lazily toying with the ends of her dark hair, while she pored over a borrowed issue of *Artists and Collectors*.

"Zenty!" Aunt Doris said. The day was Monday and for the aunts meant respite from the routine of clerking, but not—as Aunt Rhoda wryly observed—from work. Not with Doris around. "Put that magazine *away*."

"Yessum," the girl replied, but she was not really listening. The quarterly this issue held reproductions of the Teiler art collection and for Zenty—as she studied a red-

1

barn-in-autumn scene—a discovery, a hope, a dream. She let go of her hair and traced the brush strokes of the barn painting as if copying them. Three times she had scanned the text, hunting the name of the artist. None was given. But almost certainly she knew it. She could almost believe that if she stared at the barn hard enough, its doors would open and her father would appear—tall and handsome in his paint-smeared shirt that she called his Joseph's coat of many colors. She sighed softly, but then thought again that Wig Teiler would tell her whether or not the painting was signed. She could scarcely wait to ask him and had been up early, unable to sleep for excitement. Even now the time was only about seven-thirty, she guessed, for trucks were beginning to load at the bottling works next door.

The Elm Street section of Mt. St. Clare where she lived with her two aunts had once been a fashionable part of town known as Carriage Park, but neglect had long since overtaken such of the old homes that remained. Others had been torn down to make room for filling stations, parking lots, squat boxy stores, and small manufacturing plants.

The aunts claimed there was an air of history about the neighborhood. They pointed out the coach house that lingered with quaint dignity behind the bakery on the

2

street at the rear. A hitching post stood beside the curb, and beyond the bottling works a horse-watering trough served as a bird bath for the sparrows after a rain. In the Pryors' backyard, a rusted wrought iron bench leaned lopsidedly into the April-moist earth. But to Zenty—at eighteen—these relics from another century seemed only sad like Holmes's "last leaf upon the tree."

What chiefly pleased the aunts—out of necessity—was the cheap rent. Their living quarters consisted of two large bedrooms, crowded with furniture from their home; a mammoth bathroom which Aunt Rhoda said cheerfully could house polar bears in the winter because of the temperature; and the upstairs porch that substituted for a living room in mild weather when uncluttered with Doris's projects. In addition, the Pryors, an elderly couple who owned the house, permitted the aunts to use the kitchen for breakfasts and other meals, too, when the Pryors were away.

"Zen-ty!" Aunt Doris said again in exasperation. She had gray eyes under wide pale brows, drawn now into a scowl.

"Okay, okay, okay," Zenty said. Reluctantly she tucked *Artists and Collectors* under her books at the far end of the bench and opened her set of water colors. Aunt Doris wanted an original design that could be worked into a

3

stencil for the window-box fronts—though why they needed decoration escaped Zenty. She suspected her aunt of dreaming up busy work.

Doris was a tall woman—thin and large-boned—who wore slacks whenever she properly could. She sat now on the floor with legs hunched up and a box gripped between her knees as she rubbed the wood busily with the sandpaper. The other aunt—Rhoda—had perched herself on a stool with her box rested against her shins. From time to time, she tugged at her culottes which were her only concession to anything that resembled masculine dress. And as she tugged, her face, amazingly childlike for a woman of forty, puckered with brief annoyance. Suddenly she yawned—belatedly hiding the yawn behind her hand—then flexed her arm and began to complain about her sister's fussiness. Who was to notice a few bumps in the wood?

"Me," Doris said and corrected herself. "I. Now don't *you* start acting like Zenty—as if we were only parked here and rather silly to bother with window boxes and such."

Her unexpected comments often caught Zenty off guard. Startled, she flushed as Aunt Doris went on. "After all your moving about, Zenty, I should think you'd be thankful to settle down."

"Oh, let the child alone," Aunt Rhoda muttered.

4

Zenty frowned and said, "Yes, I suppose I ought." Her mother was a practical nurse, and Zenty had spent most of her growing-up years, until graduation from high school, in nursing homes and countless other places—wherever her mother happened to work. There had been, though, one whole uninterrupted year before her parents separated when Zenty had lived with them in the country, and Father had held art classes in the barn.

She was suddenly defensive. "You forget, Aunt Doris," she said, "that I always had to be ready—mentally ready —to leave when Mom's patient got better. I sort of acquired the habit of not settling in any place."

"Yes," Aunt Doris agreed, "I expect that's true."

But still only half true, Zenty admitted. Actually she did feel perpetually poised for flight. What was more, she *wanted* to. She refused to accept Carriage Park or the clinic where she worked from eleven to six as permanent in her life. And currently, though it seemed a ridiculous hope, she did hope to go away to college in the fall. By some *miracle,* she conceded, for she could scarcely afford the solitary course she was taking this year at Mt. St. Clare College.

She set down her brush, wiped her fingers on her smock, and reaching over touched the magazine as if to recharge herself with anticipation. Precisely what she expected to happen should the barn picture turn out to be her father's work she had not yet defined, but something—something tremendously good. She drew in a deep excited breath. A spring-warm breeze ruffled the newspapers and carried a yeasty smell that drifted across the yard from the bakery. The fragrance roused again memories of the house in the country—not that Mother had ever made bread in the big, clumsy kitchen but because Zenty had always felt somebody should have.

"You know what I wish?" Aunt Rhoda asked. "I wish we were acquainted with nice youngsters Zenty's age. Aren't there any at the clinic?"

"Well, let's see," Zenty said. "There are two girls who spend their Saturdays mogging around the Square with an eye out for the boys."

"Boys they know?" Aunt Doris asked.

Aunt Rhoda winked at Zenty, and Zenty said, "Not necessarily. And then there's a secretary who's fun, but she's engaged. There's a nurse who's married and talks about my visiting her, but she lives way over in the Beechwood section. And let's see. The office boy. He keeps asking me for dates, but, among other things, he murders the King's English."

"And Zenty Sper*row*," Aunt Doris said, properly accenting the last syllable, "is a snob about the King's English."

"Well, I murder it, too, sometimes," Zenty admitted, "but I know better, and he doesn't and doesn't care that he doesn't."

"Not precisely your dish of tea," Aunt Doris said. "Well, what about your rhetoric class—aside from the great Ludwig Hellman Teiler III, of course." Her faint tone of scorn at mention of Wig annoyed Zenty, and she did not answer.

Aunt Rhoda blew sandings from her box, straightened up, and gazed soberly out at the yard. "What I really wish," she said in her soft voice, "is that Zenty could go away next September."

"Oh, not *that* again!" Aunt Doris cried. "You went through the whole rigamarole last July Fourth while Zenty sat in her room filling out an application to . . . what college?"

Zenty shook her head impatiently.

"And old Mr. Pryor stood out in the yard and banged away with a cap pistol he had found in the attic. And you—" Aunt Doris spoke jerkily as she resanded a stubborn rough spot, "you spouted on and on about how Wig's father was the ideal person to approach for a student loan. He was an art collector and presumably interested in young artists. He knew the Sperrows. To hear you, anyone would have thought we were old buddy-buddies."

"I never claimed we were *buddies*," Aunt Rhoda protested gravely. "All I said was that Molly had nursed Wig the time he broke his hip. How long ago, Zenty?"

"Mmmmm. Wig was . . . fifteen. Oh, about ten years."

"That long?" Aunt Rhoda exclaimed. "Well . . ." She paused reflectively. "I still think Mr. Teiler would remember you."

"How could he not?" Aunt Doris said in mincing tones intended to mimic her sister's. "Our little Zenty was such a pretty tyke." Her voice dropped to its normal brusqueness. "No, *hon*estly, Rhoda! We went all through the whole business last summer. Wig was the big Prince Charming you told us. And wasn't he Zenty's teacher, too?"

"Not last July Fourth he wasn't," Aunt Rhoda said reasonably. "I must have been psychic if I mentioned *that.*"

Sometimes when the aunts squabbled, Zenty could barely repress her giggles, but now she was annoyed. "Wig's been mighty good to me," she said.

"All right. Have it your way," Aunt Doris said. "But if you ask me, Wig used you as an excuse for trundling off to the zoo or the carnival or a Walt Disney movie whenever he felt in the mood. However . . ." She shrugged. "Maybe you should talk to Mr. Teiler."

"It's not as if you're begging something for nothing,

Zenty," Aunt Rhoda said. "You're merely asking for a loan."

Zenty shook her head. She still remembered her days at the Teilers' with Mother. And though Zenty had been only eight then, she had sensed attitudes and emotions that an adult might have missed. And she was convinced that Mr. Teiler did not like the Sperrows—partly, perhaps, because of Mother's manner with her patients. Mom always behaved as if she were one of the family. And partly, too, because both she and Zenty had boasted of her artist-father.

"I'm so afraid," she said, "that if I were to approach Mr. Teiler, Wig would imagine I had taken his class just to get a loan."

"Oh, that's nonsense!" Aunt Rhoda exclaimed. "Why, Wig *told* you to enroll in freshman rhetoric. Remember? The day in the library?"

"Oh, yes, I remember." When did she ever forget Wig? All the telephone pads at the switchboard were lettered with his name. Wig. Ludwig Teiler. Ludwig Hellman Teiler III, with geometric flowers and one-line birds drawn around the *L. L* for love, and *L* for Ludwig.

"Lord Bountiful," Aunt Doris muttered. She crumpled a worn sheet of sandpaper and tossed it at a wastebasket, landing the wad with the aim of a one-time girl basketball player. She stood up, shook her clothes free of the sandings, and walked over to survey Zenty's design.

"Hey, spook," she said, using her one term of endearment, "you're not half bad. My, my! We're lousy with artists in the Sperrow family." She rested a hand on Zenty's shoulder. "Are you adding other colors besides the green tones?"

"A line of tomato red and a line of yellow. I'm afraid to do anything but monotones because when I use contrasting colors my designs are spotty." She snapped her paint box shut and tapped the top impatiently. "I have so much to *learn*," she wailed.

"Oh, fiddle!" Aunt Doris lifted one knee and nudged her niece in the thigh. "Go borrow a book from the library."

Zenty sighed. "Look, Aunt Doris. It's not what I *know* I don't know that worries me so much. It's what I *don't* know that I don't know . . . if you understand me."

"Vaguely," Aunt Doris conceded. "But you've got a whole lifetime ahead of you. It won't hurt you to work a year or two. Lots of youngsters have before going on to college and have profited by their maturity. Some day, your father will return with money in his jeans for your education. You'll see."

"And what with my social security . . ." Zenty said.

"Oh, stop!" Aunt Doris laughed and poked her niece

again. "You'd better run along, spook. I'll put your stuff away." She turned the design around and studied it again. "Anyway, there's always Mt. St. Clare."

Not for art, Zenty thought. The college had a crummy department. In fact, it was not even a department. But what was the use in arguing? She grabbed up her books and the magazine and hurried into her bedroom where she pulled off her smock, changed from sneakers to flats, and combed her hair. A card from her father—showing an Irish cottage—had slipped from her bulletin board and she stopped to tack the card more firmly in place. She was about to leave then when she remembered a page of her essay that she had revised the night before.

"Oh, my gosh!" she exclaimed and ran to her grandfather's old typewriter and pulled out a sheet of paper. Hastily she scanned the rewritten lines:

Always Father insisted that I sit in on his art classes but keep quieter than even the field mice in the loft. Often he read aloud from his own boyhood readings and frequently quoted the parable from St. Matthew XXV about the man who buried his talent in the ground. It was important, Father said, for us all to understand that even the meagerest talent must be cultivated and used to the glory of God or we should lose what had only been loaned to us in the first place.

Actually, talents refused to stay buried. Big or small,

they had a way of needling one. Why did not Mother and Aunt Doris understand?

From the Pryors' rooms below echoed the half-hour chime. Zenty grabbed her purse and gloves and, calling good-bye to the aunts, raced down the stairs and out into the soft morning. And she remembered what her father had once said—that not a dozen lifetimes could fulfill all the promise of an April day. Still the promise was there— warm and exciting in the gentle air. She hugged the magazine tightly under her arm and headed for class and Wig.

TWO

The class—that met at nine on Mondays, Wednesdays, and Fridays—was over at ten of ten. Once inside the school building, Zenty usually forgot time. But today as Wig lectured and she scribbled notes, the minute hand on the classroom clock moved with a perverse slowness. She caught herself straining to hear each separate click. And she thought of the memorial cafeteria where books jostled on the tables with coke bottles, crumpled straws, empty cups, and doughnut-sugared plates—and of the magazine stashed on the rack under her chair.

At length Wig's curt but pleasant voice ceased speaking. She finished a sentence with a flourishing period, laid down her pen, and flexed her fingers. All through the classroom feet shuffled. A paper rustled as someone flipped the page of a notebook. And again the minute hand clicked.

She glanced excitedly at Wig who stood, tall and blond, with his back to the class as he wrote Wednesday's assignment on the board. Now she waited for him to turn and twirl the chalk once in his fingers before tossing it onto the ledge. She loved his air of abundant vitality. He was not perhaps a truly handsome man—the planes of his face were too broad—but he had intensely blue eyes and two thoroughly masculine dimples that refused to stay hidden whether he talked or smiled.

In the moment of respite from note-taking, Zenty stretched her legs and recrossed her ankles. She had just wiggled back in her seat when she sensed more than heard the sibilant sliding of books. An instant later, the magazine slipped to the floor with a loud and startling plop. Wig jerked about and stared at his father's portrait on the cover, and briefly his eyes flickered with annoyance. Fortunately, the bell rang. Students scrambled to their feet and clattered out except for the usual half dozen or so who clustered around Wig's desk.

Suddenly sobered and unsure, Zenty bent over and hid her flushed face as she rescued the quarterly. To retrieve her books, she had almost to stand on her head, and she grumbled at the inadequate chairs with their miserly shelf for books, no left arm, and only a wide right one that ill served a left-hander like Zenty. She straightened up with her cheeks still burning and began to stack and restack her

books. She fussed with her ball point pen and pretended
to hunt through her purse.

Several times she looked up quickly, hoping Wig would
catch her eye and motion her to wait. One thing she had
learned for a certainty about Wig: He was not predictable.
Occasionally in the winter he had taken her skating or
bowling or to the movies but always spontaneously. And
she told herself she *preferred* not to fall into a regular
pattern of dating. Come September, he would return to
Yale for work on his doctorate. She dared not grow too
dependent upon him. She ought maybe to forego the
coffee sessions, except occasionally, but, of course, today
she had to wait.

At length, when all but one boy had left, she sauntered
up to Wig's desk and stood with her head half turned so
as not to appear to be listening.

Abruptly he said, "Miss Sperrow." He always called his
girl students "Miss"—even her in class—and the boys
simply by their last names without the "Mister."

She swung about, startled at his brusque tone.

"Did you have a question?" he asked, and simultaneously glanced down at his watch.

She was so taken aback, she could not at once reply.
The boy flashed her a look of sympathy. "Uh, Mr. Teiler,"
he said, "if you'd rather, I could—"

"No," Wig said, detaining him with a hand on his arm,

1 5

and then turning to Zenty. "Can your question wait until Wednesday?"

She fingered the quarterly. She had borrowed it from the doctors' lounge and had to return it this day. "Indefinitely, I guess," Zenty said. She was growing angry now.

"If it's about that," he said, nodding toward the magazine, "bring it along on Wednesday."

"I won't have it Wednesday," she said shortly. "But no matter."

He frowned, glancing from her to *Artists and Collectors* and back again as if debating.

"Oh, it's not important," Zenty said. "It's not important at all." And clutching her books and purse more tightly, she hurried away as the bell for the next class clanged through the room. Once in the empty corridor, she started to run but stopped herself when the clamor ceased. From behind her, a latecomer raced noisily past and Zenty thought, Wig will imagine those are my heels clicking— *if* he was thinking of her at all. And why should he?

Outdoors she hurried, broke into a trot, slowed, walked briskly again. If she could somehow outdistance herself, she might not have to recall that moment of surprise. She had let herself in for it, of course, by her silly imaginings of how she and Wig would sit together in the cafeteria and pore over the magazine while he answered her one important query about the barn painting. She had indulged in foolish anticipation of his pleasure as well as hers in just being together. And then like an icy snowball between the eyes came his brusqueness, the glance at his watch—almost insulting in its obviousness.

All the same she was not hurt, she reassured herself—a little humiliated at her own stupidity and terribly surprised, but not hurt.

A voice called, "Hi, Zenty!" and turning she recognized a girl whom she had known in high school.

"Oh, hi, how are you?"

"Fine, and you?"

"Fine."

Both hesitated, then the girl waved and Zenty continued her rapid retreat from the school. Once past the edge of the campus, she wondered why she had not paused longer to talk with her ex-classmate. They were barely acquainted actually, but still it would be fun to go back for a cup of coffee if the girl had time. She might not have. And they might bump into Wig. But was that not precisely what Zenty Sperrow wanted—the chance right now to snub him? Oh, subtly, but enough to impress him with her indifference.

"What indifference?" she muttered. Whom was she kidding? And anyway she did not feel actually snubbed herself—chided, rather, as if the pupil had overstepped her bounds—presumed—*expected* teacher to invite her for a chat. Well, sure, she had in a way, but darn him! Almost every class lately he had motioned her to wait and once had sent a boy after her.

"Have you a moment, Miss Sperrow?" she mimicked. And when all the other students had departed, he always laughed and said, "How about a cup of coffee, Zenty?" or "You're not in a hurry, are you, Zenty?"

It was the way he had checked the time that piqued her most, as if she were too stupid or brash to accept a simple explanation that he was rushed. He might even have broken down enough to have called her by her first name in front of another pupil. Why hadn't she simply turned on her heel and walked out instead of standing bewildered? She could never, though, deliberately appear impertinent. She could never quite forget—not in the classroom anyway—that Wig was also Instructor Teiler. Nor was *he* inclined to let anyone forget either. Darn him!

Darn herself! Why did she always have to re-enact every unpleasantness as if it had been performed on stage? An angry horn startled her, and she jumped back from the road. She had not even remembered stepping off the curb. She waited for traffic to clear and crossed to the church corner. The clock hands of St. Albans stood at five after ten, but the church clock was famously nine minutes slow and had been for fifty years, *The Clarion and Star* claimed, and declared that to correct the old timepiece would be a form of sacrilege.

That's right, Zenty. Think of everything—anything but Wig, she advised herself. Not that you will, you dope.

She stood a moment, uncertain where to go since the clinic doors did not open until nearly eleven; then wandered into the churchyard and sat down on a bench in the sunlight. Jerking the quarterly from under her books, she stared at the picture of the elder Mr. Teiler. The face hinted of Wig though the father was much heavier boned than the son. The head was leonine with thick white hair and a powerful set above massive shoulders.

She flipped the page to a portrait of Wig's mother—a delicate, fair-haired woman whose beauty had probably been romanticized by the artist. According to the article on the Teilers, she had died when Wig was seven. One could understand why he deferred to his father. *He* was the whole of Wig's family. A tough-minded man, the news story tagged the elder Mr. Teiler. His career had fallen into classic lines, taking him from office boy and draftsman to chairman of the board. After a bout of Asiatic flu in the fall, he had retired from his advertising agency.

"My mortal enemy," Zenty said to the pigeon that fluttered down among the myrtle—and astonished herself. Was she not being melodramatic, as usual? Mr. Teiler had probably forgotten she existed. And however Wig behaved toward her, she had no reason to suspect influence from his father.

Still . . . She recalled that one night recently the college faculty had dined at the Teiler home, an event reported lavishly in *The Clarion,* and just suppose that one of the professors, having noticed Zenty with Wig in the cafeteria, had joshed him about her. And suppose the elder Mr. Teiler had listened with both ears pricked up like a great big old police dog. Oh, *hon*estly! Just let Zenty unleash her imagination and in no time Wig would be absolved and his father the villain.

With a sigh she closed the magazine. In the shadow of the transept the cool dampness smelled pungently of earth and leaf mold, and there was vaguely in the air a sense of other seasons and other springtimes blended into the new spring—a timelessness that carried her momentarily away from herself. If only she would not spend her day mentally fighting with Wig.

Oh, if!

Grabbing up her belongings, she darted out of the churchyard and across the street to the switchboard.

When Zenty left the clinic that evening, the church chimes were ringing across the narrow, empty street. As always she was relieved to be free of the fusty air, the drab walls and view of window ledges with pigeon droppings that marked the municipal building. She stood a moment and listened as the chimes dwindled off for a bare instant before the clock began to strike the hour. This moment she loved, for the mellow old-world sound suddenly spread the universe far and wide. She felt all the mysterious and wonderful life that awaited her in places and people and books and music and her own paints and brushes. And there was in the voice of the bells, though she could not say how or why—through some childhood association with a dream perhaps—a promise of self-fulfillment. She *would* find the way to be herself—student, artist, and all else that potentially was Zenty.

The last solemn bong died away, and she ran down the steps, hungry now for good solid food. In this part of town, the streets were mostly deserted by six. She hurried as she headed for the Square and then as footsteps advanced swiftly behind her instinctively walked faster. Suddenly her body stiffened under a tight grip on her arms. A magazine fell at her feet, and she saw it waveringly as she swayed gently forward, propelled by the force that held her, and swayed back again. She wrenched herself around, hot with anger, and stared up into teasing blue eyes.

"Wig, you idiot!" she remonstrated. There was an unmistakable lilt in her voice. Immediately she became disconcerted, not sure how she ought to have greeted him after his rebuff of the morning. She glanced swiftly away.

"Oh, it's *you*," he said innocently. "Hi."

Deliberately then she regarded him—frowning to let him understand she was deciding whether to stay angry or not. He looked back at her with the exaggerated gravity of a man amused. He had heard the brief note of joy and was not deceived.

"Well?" he said with humble inquiry that really was not very humble, she guessed.

"You're not supposed to go around scaring people. Outside the classroom," she added.

"Do I scare anyone *inside* the classroom?" he asked.

"I wouldn't know," she said and then quickly, to change the subject, "Are you just coming from school?"

"*No!*" He nodded toward the churchyard. "I've been hunting ancestors among tombstones. Here, feel." He touched her hand, and his fingers were cold. She was so startlingly aware of him that for a moment she stood unmoving. He was silent, too, contemplating her in the smoky April evening.

She heard herself say, "Why?" and the word broke the mood.

"Why what?" he asked.

"Hunt ancestors until you're chilled? They won't run away."

"Oh, *that*." He laughed. "I guess you're right. Well, you see, my father's on a genealogical binge again. Only he ought not to potter about in damp graveyards. So occasionally I take on the assignment." He stooped to retrieve the magazine that had dropped. Her heart jumped as she saw *Artists and Collectors* and caught a glimpse of Mr. Teiler's white hair. Had Wig really been searching out ancestors' names on tombstones or waiting for Zenty Sperrow? She knew what she wanted to believe all right, all right, but with Wig one could never be sure.

"Look, I'm famished," he said. "How about you? Shall we have dinner?" He spoke casually as if the idea had just occurred to him. And maybe it had.

She surveyed the expensive lines of his tweed coat. All day she had felt end-of-winter shabby in her blue-and-rose striped blouse and her blue suit that never stayed thoroughly brushed.

He cocked an eyebrow at her. "Or have you a date?"

"By now," she said, "there are so many messages waiting for me, I shall have to toss them into a hat and draw out one."

"Fancy that."

"Mmmmm. Hmmmm," she said nodding, "but I guess I won't bother. I'll just go along with you."

"Mighty decent of you."

She nodded again. Mighty foolish, too. What did he

expect of her—that she be available whenever he desired to see her but stay unobtrusive when he did not? Or had she a chip on her shoulder? Mother said she had, and maybe she was right.

"Now what are you scowling about?" Wig asked.

"Am I scowling?"

"Yes, you are, and doing yourself an injustice, you know. Call the aunts from the restaurant, if that's what's worrying you."

He slipped her arm through his and pressed her hand firmly against the sleeve of his coat. Sometimes as now he could be disarmingly protective. She wondered why tonight she felt momentarily depressed as if she had guessed something about their relationship that she did not really want to know. He was an old friend and her teacher and, all right, she had fallen in love with him—a *little*. She had imagined herself in love before, for mercy's sake, and survived.

"You'd enjoy a shore restaurant, wouldn't you?" Wig asked. "We're only half an hour away once we find the car." He glanced along the street. "Oh, there it is."

He motioned toward a low sleek green model that appeared newly washed and polished. A soft cashmere coat with a gay scarf—not too dressy—would look smart in the seat next to the driver. As she approached the car, the mellowing sun, reflecting off the side mirror, winked into

her eyes. The sudden blinding light was so like a rebuking
nudge that she almost laughed aloud. Wig opened the
door for her and made certain she was settled before he
closed it again, and once more she had the sense of being
cared for that he managed to convey in a way unlike any
other young man she had ever known. She felt now so
contented that she wondered what had ailed her all day.
She did fuss altogether too much.

THREE

The restaurant had red-and-white tablecloths and thick candles in bottles over which melted wax in many colors had dripped and hardened. There was a pleasant mingling of herbs and garlic and charcoal broiling in the air. Wig checked his coat but brought *Artists and Collectors* to the table and slid it onto a vacant chair, but he did not mention the magazine nor did she for fear of evoking the morning's encounter. There the quarterly remained like Banquo's ghost, making them suddenly constrained. Wig, in fact, appeared preoccupied. Once he sighed, and when she asked about his doctor's thesis which he was working on this year at home, he merely shook his head at her. Perhaps he had run into snags but she wished he would talk about them because then maybe some of his problems would straighten out. She wished she could help him.

Then the food arrived and they commented on the variety: melon, minestrone, salad, great hunks of Italian bread, cheese, pickled relishes, black olives, celery, a side dish of spaghetti, oysters brochette for her, and shad roe for Wig. He insisted that she taste it and watched for her reaction. She had noticed before how he enjoyed *her* enjoyment of whatever he had made possible—whether it was her first glimpse of circus riders or as now her first taste of a new dish. Of course, why should he not? Except . . . well . . . Aunt Doris's remarks had unsettled Zenty's childhood acceptance of Wig, and she wondered now whether *he* thought of himself as Indulgent Big Brother Wig—in capital letters.

Musing, she ate slowly. By now she had overcome her early adolescent self-consciousness that was due to the many mentors in her life—grandmothers, wives, maiden aunts of her mother's patients, hospital staff.

"Do you know," she said to Wig, hoping to amuse him, "when I was ten and living in the Mt. St. Clare Nursing Home with Mother, I practiced two sets of table manners?"

"Only two?" Wig asked. "I'm sure I had a dozen and all atrocious."

"Just two," Zenty said. "One for the kitchen where I drank cocoa with the spoon in the cup because cook never bothered with saucers. 'Don't be such a little tiddler,' she'd

27

say. And another set for the dining room where the head nurse kept an eye on me all the time. Funny how kids adjust."

"Very," he agreed solemnly. He always listened interestedly, but tonight she had again a sense of indulgence. Or—it suddenly occurred to her that the dinner was a kind of unspoken apology on Wig's part and that he expected her in some way to respond, to show her understanding that anyone might have reasons for being curt sometimes. He might have been unusually harassed.

After forming and rejecting several sentences in her mind, she asked, "Did you have a terribly busy day?"

He straightened up, visibly rousing, flashed her a broad smile, and said, "Yes, rather." He had decided suddenly to join the party, Zenty thought. "I spent the morning looking at high school records. You certainly moved around a lot, didn't you? I knew you had, of course, but I didn't realize how often. You must have changed schools about every year, didn't you?"

"Sometimes twice a year. I suppose you noticed grades, too?"

"Why, sure," he told her cheerfully. "Yours are a mixed bag all right enough, and you're such a good student, Zenty. What made you goof off? The constant moving?"

"Oh, no, I guess I can't blame that altogether," Zenty said. She set the salt cellar on a red square of the tablecloth and the pepper on the white square as if lining up chessmen. "We rarely stayed anywhere long enough for me to make many friends. So I read a lot, and it was easier just to read silly stories than to do algebra, especially since I hate arithmetic."

"Glad I'm not teaching arithmetic," Wig said.

"So am I." She hesitated and then added, "You're tough," and it occurred to her that he rather liked to believe himself so.

"Oh, come now," Wig said.

"Well, you are. But you enjoy teaching, don't you?" He nodded, and she said, "All the papers though—don't you mind correcting them?"

"Oh, sometimes. But they tell me a great deal about my students. You'd be surprised how much." He raised his eyebrows at her.

"So that's why you assign autobiographical sketches," she said. "No fair. You cheat."

"Why, I do not. I don't like cheaters any better than you do."

"Now you've got me worried," she told him. "What else do you know about me besides the fact that I don't like cheaters?"

He looked at her closely and then said, "That you're a rare spirit." She felt her color rising and with it a sudden rush of happiness.

"Oh," she murmured and heard him sigh again, so softly she could not be altogether sure he had. Compliments made her shy, and she shifted the conversation quickly away from herself. "I'll bet your father's pleased that you're teaching this year."

Wig squinted at his coffee cup, twirled it round by the handle and back again. "Not . . . noticeably," he said.

"Oh, well, I just meant pleased that you're home."

"Well, that, yes." He grimaced and laughed shortly. "Can you picture me at the Court of St. James?"

"At *what?*"

"With ambassadorial ribbons across my chest or whatever it is ambassadors wear to distinguish themselves?"

She was briefly puzzled and then said, with an attempt at Cockney English, "Oh, Saynt Jaymes. In London. As ambassador to Britain?" She pretended to reflect. "Mmmmm. Yes," she said with a nod.

"So can my father." Wig drummed angrily on the table.

"What do you have to do to become an ambassador?" she asked.

"I don't know and couldn't care less," he said savagely. "*Professor* Teiler will satisfy me. One does not acquire a professorship overnight either."

She had never heard him admit to being at odds with his father over anything. She was beginning to wonder whether she really knew Wig at all.

Suddenly he chuckled. "Pardon my snarling," he said.

"Actually Father means well, and, of course, I'm the only son he has."

"All the same," Zenty said, "I do wish people wouldn't try to pigeonhole."

"Sometimes you startle me, Zenty," he said, "with your observations. Oh, by the way." He lifted *Artists and Collectors* onto the table. His eyes narrowed, and one dimple deepened in his cheek as he concentrated on flattening the magazine. A faint warmth rose into her throat as the incident of the morning flashed through her mind. She stared intently at his hands with their squared palms and long fingers as she wondered how she could shift the conversation adroitly so that the question she had intended to ask might now appear unrelated to their earlier encounter.

"Did you notice my mother's portrait?" he asked.

"Yes. She must have been very lovely. I read about your father, too, and all the arguments he has with the critics on draftsmanship and art."

"Oh-yes-oh-yes," Wig said. "Unless a man is a good draftsman, he is no artist. Unquote."

"Do you have to sound so scornful?" Zenty asked.

"A lot of rubbish."

"Not altogether," she said indignantly.

Wig regarded her in astonishment. "What are you so excited about?" he asked.

"I suppose you belong to the smear-and-dab school," she

said. "I suppose good draftsmanship can't possibly be art."

"You look as if you'd like to bite," he observed. "Here." He reached across and held his hand close to her mouth. She leaned away and repressed a smile.

"Oh, I see," he said softly. "Arnold Sperrow, eh?"

There was no smile to hide now, only a quick anger. She pressed her lips tightly to hold it back. Always when Wig mentioned her father, he spoke—how could she say? —not precisely with a note of derision but with a concealment of it that one could nevertheless sense. Wig's attitude probably was a hangover from childhood when undoubtedly the Teilers had joked between themselves about the Sperrows' boasting. Admittedly, Zenty was oversensitive. But she felt frustrated in being unable to defend Father for the very reason that no criticism or even skepticism of his artistry was actually expressed. One could not set up the straw men and then knock them down oneself.

She stared out at the lights, noting that where they reflected long in the water, the waves heaved slowly, rhythmically, like a creature breathing deeply in sleep.

Wig said gently, "Well, here, let me show you a painting that I believe *is* art and excellent draftsmanship, too." He flipped the pages to the center spread of reproductions while Zenty held her breath, waiting. It would be ironic if he chose the picture she believed to be her father's.

"Yes, here we are," Wig said, pointing to the red barn

in an autumn landscape that had the crispness and delicacy of a fall day when only the last scattered drops of color clung to the trees. "The reproduction doesn't show up the detail as well as the original, of course, but the brush work is magnificent."

How well she knew, for had she not copied the very picture and others, too, in the barn itself? Or thought she had.

"All the same," Wig said, "it is not the brush work nor the texture nor color nor composition that make the picture art—at least in my untutored opinion—but the spirit that the artist has caught. For me, this is not just *an* autumn landscape but what I feel about certain autumn days, year after year."

She listened impatiently, for she was more agitated than she wished Wig to guess, and she had to control her voice before she spoke.

"Who is the artist?" she asked, and waited tensely for Wig's reply.

"We don't know. Can you imagine? The painting is unsigned."

Oh, but it was not, she thought. Somewhere in the right-hand corner among the clump of fallen leaves, she would bet the outline of a sparrow nestled. If she could see the original, somewhere she would find a sparrow— the arrogant signature on her father's work, though he usually painted his initials on the reverse side of a canvas, too.

"Is there nothing on the back of the painting?" she asked.

"Another view of the barn—and down in the corner a date. It's recent, you know. The painting was done four or five years ago."

Yes. She was thirteen when the Sperrows had tried their experiment of taking a house in the country. She was fourteen when the experiment failed. Sometimes it seemed incredible that she could not go back and find Father standing, perhaps in the barn doorway, debonair and paint-dabbed. He would bawl out to her in his voice that might easily have been an actor's and demand to know what she had done with his vermilion or his finest sable brush that he claimed to have brought from Hong Kong. Silly, but she was actually trembling inside.

"My father," Wig said, *"thinks* he bought the picture at a sidewalk exhibit, but he's not sure, and he can't remember where—Greenwich Village, Paris, maybe."

"Or Mt. St. Clare?" Zenty asked.

"I'm afraid not," Wig told her. "Our local talent isn't equal to this." His eyes twinkled at her. "We except your father, of course."

Some day, Ludwig Hellman Teiler III was going to be

set back on his heels, but not until she was sure of her discovery. She would have to see the original barn painting. But how?

Wig stared musingly at his cup and then said, "No, wait. I retract what I said about local talent. How could I forget Giuseppe? Half the time he's out in left field, of course, but even so, I ought to tell him." Wig tipped back his sleeve and glanced at his watch. Involuntarily she stiffened and at once was annoyed with herself that she could not forget her slighted feelings of the morning.

"Who is Giuseppe?" she asked.

"A friend of mine—as I expect you've gathered. Terrific guy and a fine artist."

"Guess I don't know him."

"No, but you will," Wig promised. "In fact, we may stop to see him on our way home. He has a shack down on the shore where he lives in spring and summer while he finishes out the teaching year—and later paints and fishes and gets away from his family's togetherness."

"Funny," Zenty said, "some families have too much and others haven't any at all."

Once more she stared out at the water where lights silhouetted a boat moving along the horizon. On shore, a bonfire flamed and now and then faces ruddy with the glow drifted into view and away again. When she turned back, Wig was watching her intently with an expression that Aunt Rhoda described as the look-of-a-man-with-a-maid. Almost at once it disappeared.

He walked around the table and pulled back her chair. His arm reached about her shoulders as he helped her on with her coat, and he did not immediately let go. Once again she heard his almost inaudible sigh. She could not say why it depressed her.

FOUR

The tide had turned, and, no longer somnolent, broke in frisky waves that reached closer and closer inshore. At the end of Good King's Point, the lighthouse glistened whitely, and the beam sweeping across the water passed over bits of flying spray and then left them to the night again.

Wig parked the car in a public lot at the end of a quiet street leading to the beach. The air had the spring-freshness of April—a mingling of tanginess and seaweed and new growth. With only the sighing of the sea and the noise of an occasional pebble kicked along the path, there was about the night an other-world quality, something not quite real or not quite ordinary.

Guided by Wig's flashlight, Zenty followed him down a stony trail toward the shore and Giuseppe's place.

"What do you say we go barefoot?" Wig asked.

"Are you joking?"

He laughed in the darkness. "No, I'm not, little Miss Proper."

"But what will your friend think if we appear at his door in our bare feet?"

"He'll be *de*-lighted, especially if he's banging around in old rags."

"All right then," Zenty said.

She and Wig sat back to back on the rocks. When she had rolled her stockings together, she tucked them into her shoes. Wig reached for her hand, and with him she picked her way gingerly over the pebbles and onto the sand. It was cool underfoot and gave Zenty a sense of childlike ease. She watched Wig's feet beside hers as they moved in and out of the glow of his flashlight. His big toes were shorter than the second ones—as she had read Napoleon's were. And what did they make Wig, she asked him—a tyrant or a genius?

"A guy with long second toes," he told her.

She stopped and hung onto his shoulder to steady herself while she brushed a stone from the sole of her foot. At that moment, she felt right and comfortable with Wig as if the peacefulness of the night had calmed all her mercurial emotions of the day.

Sometimes she liked to believe that fate had led Wig to the library at the very hour she and Aunt Rhoda had stopped in to look over the college catalog, but, of course, nothing so occult had happened unless one could call Aunt Rhoda fate. She was forever overhearing gossip in the art store where she clerked. In fact, Aunt Doris claimed all the place lacked were cracker and pickle barrels and a nineteenth-century stove. Anyway, weeks before enrollment there had been talk that young Wig Teiler was to teach freshman rhetoric in the fall and also that he was working on his doctorate and used the library on certain mornings. And so it was Aunt Rhoda who had steered Zenty, all unknowing, there at the time. And perhaps there was an element of fate in the doing after all, for whenever Zenty suspected maneuvering in her affairs, she invariably rebelled.

Zenty shifted her weight and brushed the sole of her other foot. The searchlight traveled to her face, and she blinked.

"Just checking to see if I still have a girl with me or a ghost," Wig said. "Look, there's Giuseppe beaching his boat." He shouted loudly enough to startle her, "Hi ya, Gyps."

A dark figure at the shore straightened up. He had a lantern in his hand, and as he waved it, Zenty caught a flash of red. Giuseppe whistled a long complicated trill, and Wig replied. As she and Wig neared the shack which was built on stilts, Giuseppe exclaimed in a mock Southern accent, "Frah ma hide iffen it ain't the admiral hisself."

"Been promoted, have I?" Wig remarked, and then told Zenty, "Gyps and I were in boot camp together in North Carolina, and he has never recovered from the South."

"Please, cap'n, suh," Gyps said, "Not *North* Carolina. *Up* Carolina."

"That joke's older than you are," Wig said. "Now behave, will you? I've brought a lady to meet you."

"Blimey!" Gyps said, discarding his Southern role. "Let us repair to my disordered abode." He held the lantern to guide Zenty up the steps. "Boot camp," he said in disgust. "*I* was in boot camp. He was a j.g., lower than which you cannot get."

He opened a door that showed weather blisters where the lantern struck it. At once, Wig reached in and flipped a switch. Zenty closed her eyes briefly against the harsh glare while Gyps let out an outraged yelp.

"Please," he said plaintively, lighting an oil lamp on a round table by a slightly disheveled sofa. He hung the lantern, still lit, by the door, and flicked the switch, leaving the room to mellow light and deep shadows. "Better," he said, pleased.

Zenty thought how ridiculous she and Wig must appear, standing, both of them, with shoes in their hands. But Wig, unconcerned, introduced Giuseppe Di Costa to her.

She said, "How do you do," and saw now that Gyps was a remarkably handsome man, slightly taller than Wig, with medium brown hair, dark eyes, and heavy lashes. A red flannel shirt gave his skin a warm glow. She had a notion then that she had met him before. He stood quite still and frankly appraised her, and she was suddenly shy under his gaze.

Abruptly he said with a softness she found further disconcerting, "Ah, so. I had heard rumors." Out of the tail of her eye, she saw Wig's startled turn of the head. "And now I understand why you have been absent of late. I'm afraid I must forgive you, Captain."

"I'm confused," Zenty said, truthfully enough. "What are you, Wig? Captain or j.g.?"

"I came out of the Navy a lieutenant commander," Wig said, "but all is forgotten now."

"But not forgiven," Gyps said. "No. No, never. But sit, sit." He passed his hand quickly over the rumpled coverlet on the day bed. "I'll take the rocking chair, and if I advance upon you in my furious preoccupation with this charming company, do not be alarmed."

Zenty sat primly with both bare feet together on the wood floor, and Wig, with a jerk at his pants legs, lowered himself beside her.

"*Scusate. Un momento,*" Gyps said and disappeared into the shadows where presently the light from an opened refrigerator outlined a doorway and shone on an oilcloth table top.

"Gyps," Wig called after his friend, "we have just come from an enormous dinner."

"Si, si, signore. No food. I understand."

"No anything, you mug."

"Ah, speak for yourself, John Smith. The lady . . ." His words disappeared in clinking noises, and a moment later he returned with coke bottles. Setting one down beside Zenty, he said, "Oh, yes, for the lady a glass—preferably a *clean* glass. Now where? Ah." He pulled open a drawer in the round table and brought forth straws in their wrappings. "I knew I was saving these for some reason, and a prettier one I can't imagine."

She laughed, and saw that Wig was watching her. "You do make handsome speeches," she told Gyps.

He ignored the rocking chair after all and sank down onto the floor near Zenty's feet and hugged his knees to him. He and Wig began to talk then—about waterproof paints and stuff for caulking boats and mutual friends and the elder Mr. Teiler's health. Much improved, Wig said, though he still worried about his father . . . some.

Gyps ran his tongue from the inside of one cheek to the other, speculatively. "You're returning to Yale this fall?"

"I guess so," Wig said.

Gyps lowered his chin until it touched his knees and

scowled up at Wig. "What do you mean, you guess so?
Look, Teiler, you're not sort of half planning to twiddle
around for another year, are you now?"

Wig muttered under his breath, then said aloud, "What
do you mean, twiddle around? The first draft of my thesis
will be finished by Christmas. Does that sound as if I'm
twiddling around?"

"Mmmmm. Don't know."

"Confound you! Have you ever tried to please a bunch
of dogmatic eggheads—each with a different notion about
what you ought to do or more specifically what you ought
not to do?"

"No, but a lot of guys have. And I just keep wondering
why you're postponing that degree."

"I am not postponing anything," Wig rasped. "I have
not *been* postponing anything."

"All right. All right. All *right.*" Gyps turned to Zenty.
"Don't mind us. We take the hide off each other reg-
ularly."

"And that reminds *me,*" Wig said. "Do you still have
that boat painting hanging around—the one that *looks*
like boats?"

"Maybe. Why?"

"Well, I'll tell you: My father is—how shall I say it?—
sponsoring an art contest with a thousand dollars as first
prize."

Gyps whistled, and Zenty braced her feet against the floor and sat up suddenly straight and listening.

"And if you'll be reasonable for a change," Wig said, "you can probably win. I mean win honestly. I'm not offering to pull strings, you understand. Just that you could, hands down. Only you know my father's feelings about nonobjective art. He intends to be one of the judges himself, and his influence . . . well, he's the guy who's paying the bill, so . . ."

Gyps jumped to his feet and padded around the room. "Ah, pickles," he said.

"Now wait a minute, boy," Wig said. "No one's asking you to compromise your precious integrity. You're an artist no matter what you paint."

"The heck I am," Gyps said.

"A lousy stubborn mule, but an artist," Wig said. "What's wrong with entering one of your earlier pieces— or a new one so long as it's representational? Look at Picasso. He tried his hand at everything, though, come to think of it, I doubt that Picasso could win in my father's show. No, seriously, Gyps, don't be pigheaded." His hands hung between his knees as he regarded his friend earnestly. "Look, how long would it take you to get your master's if you didn't have to earn a living for a while?"

Gyps shrugged. "A year, I suppose. When's this here exhibition coming off?"

"Sometime in May."

"That's late for enrolling in a school—if, say, I won and did decide to go on."

"Yes," Wig agreed, "but what do you want to bet my father would get you enrolled somewhere?"

"Yeah, but where? In a school of your father's choice?"

Wig reached over and pounded Gyps lightly on the arm. "Boy-o-boy, you don't look a gift horse *just* in the mouth, do you?"

"No, I like to be sure he doesn't sag in the middle either."

Slowly Zenty leaned back into the shadows, afraid to betray her own eagerness. Her heart pounded as if she had been running uphill a long, long time. And in a sense she had—with still a far piece to go. Had she any chance at all to win the contest? She supposed Mr. Teiler, as the most important judge of the paintings, would intend to be fair. But all sorts of subconscious prejudices would influence his decision—as they would anyone's. She wished she were not so sure that he disliked the Sperrows. And here she was, defeating herself before the contest even opened.

Stupid!

In her preoccupation, she curled the toes of her right foot over her left.

Gyps said, "Maybe I'll paint Zenty."

"With three eyes?" Wig inquired, resting his hand on her arm as if to claim her. "Not on your life."

"Three gorgeous eyes and two cute noses. By the way, is Zenty your real name?"

"No. My father nicknamed me Zenty so that I wouldn't be called Cass or Andy or Sandy."

"Huh?" Gyps blinked at her. "You've lost me."

"My *mother* named me Cassandra."

"Fond of Greek mythology, is she?" Gyps asked.

"My mother? No. Soap opera. Cassandra was her favorite heroine. And then, since Mother is provident, she made sure my initials would spell a word because, see, if your initials spell a legitimate word, you're bound to be rich."

"Blimey! Had I but known. So what's your full name?"

"Cassandra Uhlman Sarah Sperrow."

Gyps nodded knowingly to Wig. "Cuss Sperrow."

"And she can be," Wig said slyly, "when the lady's annoyed."

She flushed, wondering whether he referred to her reactions that morning, and she said quickly, "Do you have your boat picture here, Gyps?"

"Oh, yes, the boat picture," Wig said. "I still want to buy it, Gyps." Zenty tucked her feet under her on the sofa, relieved to have the spotlight shifted away from her.

"I've told you a dozen times," Gyps said to Wig. "The picture is not for sale. I'll give it to you, but I will not—"

"Stop being a mule."

"On second thought, I will not give it to you either—not until after the contest. I do not trust you, me lad, *not* to take matters into your own hands."

Wig gazed at Gyps blankly.

"Yeah, I know that expression," Gyps said. "You're a low-down schemer, but you will not enter any picture of mine in your father's exhibition—not without my express permission. Understand?"

"Are you sure you haven't a Dutch ancestor somewhere?"

"Oh, Italians can be independent, too."

"Stubborn is the word."

"That's as may be," Gyps said. "I'm curious, though, about this contest. What put the idea into your father's head, anyway?"

"Heck, he's always been interested in the arts, hasn't he?"

"Yeah," Gyps agreed. "In a limited way."

"Now, see here, boy," Wig said heatedly. As he had once told Zenty, he could criticize his father but let no one else try. "There *are* a few connoisseurs still left who look on Holbein and Rembrandt as artists, you know. What if my father is a classicist?"

"Oh, tut, tut. Temper, temper," Gyps said. "I only mean . . . Well, something is nagging at the back of my crude mind. Hasn't your father been feuding lately about whether or not draftsmen are artists?"

"Yes, in a way."

"So now he's looking for some kid to prove his point, some young draftsman with imagination to promote, huh?"

"You louse," Wig said.

"Stinking," Gyps agreed amiably. "I get these nasty little thoughts from time to time. Only, see, if that *is* the gambit, then I may as well spare my efforts."

"You can win if you choose to," Wig said, "and if you are not too plagued lazy to try."

"Well, well, don't think I don't appreciate all this. I do. Indeed, I do."

"Then prove it," Wig said. His hand slid along Zenty's arm and closed over her fingers. "We have to be shoving off," he said, and rising, pulled her gently to her feet.

Gyps groaned in protest and once outside managed to delay Wig further while they inspected the caulking on Gyps's boat, but at last Zenty and Wig broke away. From down the beach, Wig circled his flashlight twice, and farther along still, they sat down on the rocks to put on shoes and hose. In silence, then, Wig and Zenty climbed the slight incline to the street. As they walked toward the parking lot, it seemed to Zenty that Wig was troubled. He opened the car door for her and then stood beside her a moment as they both gazed off toward the sea.

A crescent moon with a baby star just beyond the tip sailed clear of a frail cloud and shed the mysterious brightness of moonlight on sky and water below. Along the beach, patches of wet sand glistened, and even the disheveled heaps of abandoned seaweed cast their ragged shadows. And now the beam from Good King's Point—wispy with mist—swept with measured speed across the waves. Wig, still unspeaking, stared down at her and smiled, and she felt a closeness to him, intimate and sweet. But almost at once she reminded herself to be wary. Better to love her paints and brushes and the whole vast world of nature that waited to be captured on canvas. Better to love books and music. They never failed her unless she failed them. She sighed deeply.

Wig said, "As bad as all that?"

"Not bad at all," she said. "It's been a lovely evening."

"I should hope you'd think so," Wig said. "You've made a conquest, you know."

She wished he had said, "another conquest," but he had not. She pulled in the corner of her coat as Wig closed the car door. She waited until he had walked around to the driver's seat and settled himself behind the wheel.

"Gyps is colorful," she said.

"He's a great guy, but sometimes I could kick him. He's so blasted independent, no one can help him."

"Does he need help?"

"Well, yes," Wig said, as if surprised by the question. "I think so. Right now he's teaching in a private school that doesn't pay much, and he contributes to his parents' support. They live with a married sister, and I guess all the brothers and sisters contribute something, but they have big families. And so . . ." He turned on the ignition and started the engine. "Another year of schooling would make a tremendous difference to Gyps if only . . ." He lapsed into silence.

And Zenty thought, yes, a lot of difference if only Gyps cared, but he did not. And she did. Almost anyone, she supposed, would say that Gyps needed the education more than she because college degrees meant larger pay checks. As if one measured the desirability of an education in dollars and cents. For her it was a stimulant like the plant food Aunt Doris fed her potted begonias to make them grow full and abundant.

The car left the streets along the beach and ran now through farmland where here and there moonlight gleamed on a weathercock or reflected in a barn window. The shadows of trees lay long and grotesque, and the peepers piped loudly in the night. She felt again as earlier in the day a sense of the world's wideness and wonder that was almost an ache.

Now Wig spoke as if continuing a train of thought aloud. "I'm afraid that Gyps has hit on something though. Father probably isn't altogether altruistic about this art contest. I shouldn't be surprised if he was planning to find some kid who has the kind of talent Father admires and make an artist of him."

"Oh, Wig, you can't select someone and say, 'Now you're going to be an artist,' and presto he's an artist."

"If you start with the right fellow you can, and Father's pretty shrewd." Wig was smiling now and shortly he began to chuckle. "I wish Gyps would sell me a couple of his paintings. I'd pay him enough so that he could enroll next fall. It would be rather exciting to match my boy against Father's."

"*Wig!*" she exclaimed.

"Now, see here, young lady," he said. "Anybody who makes snide remarks about her mother's being a soap opera fan better not criticize me for a little good-natured rivalry with my parent."

But it was not the rivalry that had shocked her but rather Wig's possessive and—well—sort of superior way of referring to Gyps. What had Aunt Doris called Wig? Lord Bountiful?

"So I'm chided," Zenty said absently, and, unthinking, added, "for the second time today."

Wig laughed. "I wondered when you would get around to *that,*" he said. "You *were* annoyed, weren't you? Well, you'll have to forgive me, Zenty. Father and I had a yak session last night, and I was in a foul mood this morning —not that that's any excuse. Only I was, and rushed besides."

He fell quiet then as if remembrance had depressed him, and for a time they rode along silently while she mused on the contest and wondered whether or not women were excluded.

At length she said, "Wig."

"Yes."

"Are there—uh—limitations as to who may enter your father's art exhibit? I mean restrictions as to age—or anything?"

"Not that I know of. If you mean—is Gyps too old to qualify—no, I'm sure not."

Well, she would just have to wait and see. If women were not allowed to participate, she still had a sort of general plan now. First, to discover whether the barn painting in the Teiler collection was her father's work . . . then somehow to convince the elder Mr. Teiler that she was worth the risk of a student loan. She would make clear *at once* that she wanted nothing free. She could be independent, too, and meant to be. She would have to explain that her grades were not scholarship level, but Wig could vouch for her as a student. And she did have artistic talent thanks to her father, and, thanks to his sporadic coaching, she was ready for art school, if not college. She hoped the barn painting—if it was her father's work— would convince Mr. Teiler.

Oh, no more wishing and dreaming tonight, she told herself firmly. She drew in a long breath of the cool air and said to Wig, "Look how high the moon is. Are we very late?"

"Not very, no. Is there any special hour when the old sorority house locks up?"

"You mean the Etta Bitta Pi House?" she asked.

"*Zen-*ty! You're as corny as Gyps."

"Disgusting," she agreed, "and not even original. Well, anyway, I have a key, remember? And the aunts leave a night light on until they hear the pitter-patter of my sneaking feet in the upper hall. I sort of wish they wouldn't—the aunts, I mean."

"I'm glad they do," Wig said.

Ahead, the car lights flashed on a sign that read WELCOME TO MT. ST. CLARE. Behind it, the woods that skirted the town lay in mysterious darkness. She glanced above the treetops and said, "I wish I could wish on the new moon. But I can't remember whether to look over my right or left shoulder. One is lucky, and the other unlucky, and I can't recall which, can you?"

"If I could, I wouldn't tell you unless I knew what you were wishing for."

"Oh, that's easy. I'm wishing for an *A* in freshman rhetoric, naturally." The moment she had spoken, she gasped silently and bit her tongue so hard it hurt.

"So that's why you went to dinner with me, eh?"

"Oh, Wig, no! I don't know why I said anything so stupid."

"My remark wasn't very smart either," he admitted.

"Wig, believe me, please, I wouldn't like you so mu—" She caught herself up sharply. "Very much," she amended, "if—"

"Why don't you say what you mean?"

". . . If I thought you played favorites. I admire integrity. I do, honestly."

"Yes, I know you do, Zenty. And I wouldn't like you so mu—very much—if you didn't."

She giggled at his mimicry of her. The car turned along her street where the few remaining old houses still retained a dignity at night when darkness hid their disrepair and weather-beaten paint and muddy gardens. Just beyond the street lamp, he helped her from the car and walked up the worn steps to the front door. He opened it with her key and reached in to switch on the hall light. Then he held out *Artists and Collectors.*

"Would you like to keep this?" he asked. "Father got a few complimentary copies."

"Oh, yes," she said eagerly. "Yes, I would." He tucked the magazine under her arm. "Got it?" he asked.

She nodded, and he stood very close to her, hesitating. She swayed toward him and started to whisper, "Oh, Wig, I love you."

Then abruptly he said, "Be seeing you," and whistling softly ran down the steps and hurried toward his car.

Inside the house, she closed the door and leaned against it. She was shaken by the words that had almost spoken themselves. She was headed for hurt, and she did not see how she could stop herself now.

She ran quietly on upstairs to her room and pulled from her desk a magnifying glass that her grandfather had used for reading the fine print of old newspapers in libraries. She flipped open the magazine to the Teiler art collection and, holding it toward the light, examined the barn painting under the glass.

After a few moments, she straightened up with a faint sigh. She just could not be sure, and yet she was. Half hidden in the clump of leaves on the right was—something. It *had* to be the Sperrow sparrow.

5 5

FIVE

On the following Sunday, Zenty started out for her weekly
visit to her mother. Mrs. Sperrow currently worked at the
Kohlmans', whose youngest son, Horace, was recovering
from a gland infection. He was a precocious boy of about
nine whom Zenty enjoyed even though he was tempera-
mental—arrogant on his "well" days, frightened and pathetic on his poor ones.

As she buckled her red raincoat against the drizzle and
stepped off the rain-soaked porch, she thought with anticipation of the child and hoped he would beg her to read
as he often did. It always amazed Zenty that a spoiled
child, half her age, could be companionable and stimulating. And why? Because already he loved the language
as deeply as she did. They were, to paraphrase an old
poem, students of their sweet English tongue.

Yet frequently her visits depressed her, for she knew her mother desired an intimacy of thought with her daughter that simply did not exist between them. Always she promised herself that *this* Sunday there would be no squabbles. No matter what Mother said, Zenty would not contradict her, would not take offense. And always she did.

She stood now for a moment at the gate while she tied her plastic scarf tighter. Deserted and gray this chill Sunday, Elm Street had the forlorn air of the unkempt. As she started away from the house, she remembered what her father had once told her—that she used beauty as a narcotic, drugging herself with it. Ugliness, he maintained, often had a magnificence of its own. Ugliness, yes, she agreed, but shoddiness and litter, no. And she hated the negligence and indifference that caused them. Today, she felt more impatient than ever to escape, as if drabness would imprison her if she did not soon break away.

She hurried along in the rain, skipping over puddles where an accumulation of papers and cigarette butts had clogged the drains. Farther on, she crossed over the tracks of an abandoned railroad spur. Now as she neared the public library with its massive, carved stone books that rested one on either side of the stone stairway, she began to run, relishing the wetness of the mist on her face. She pretended that she was hurrying home where she would find a fire burning in the book-lined den and the tea things set out on a cart.

Behind her, a horn honked, but she did not turn until a familiar green car pulled up and waited beside a copper beech, rain-drenched and nubby with fat buds.

"Hi," Wig called to her, and got out of the car as she approached. "Going my way, lady?"

In spite of her excitement at seeing Wig, she was suddenly cautious. "Maybe," she said. "Which is your way?"

"Up to the Kohlmans' to say hello to Mrs. Sperrow."

Zenty hesitated. Of course, he had known Mother for ten years now, and there was no reason why he should not drop in to talk with her. Only somehow, Zenty feared he might complicate what was always a touchy affair.

"Hey, that rhymes," Wig said. "Hello to Mrs. Sperrow."

"Mmmmm. Hmmmm," Zenty said. "And will the class please note that rhyming prose is not considered good form."

"Stop throwing my words back at me and hop in," Wig said. She let him settle her in the car and sat frowning as he walked around and climbed in beside her. "I can stay only a few minutes. Dad's got a dinner date fixed up with old clients of his."

She was so aware of his nearness that she could scarcely refrain from touching him.

"You have rain on your eyelashes," he told her. "Come

to think of it, I believe I *am* glad you're with me. How would I find my way alone?"

"As if you had any intention of going alone," she said, and held her thumbnail between her teeth. Then realizing that she might appear to be chewing her fingernails, she dropped her hand into her lap. "You turn left at the corner," she directed, "and follow straight on to Pepperidge Lane."

She relaxed then and, trying not to fret, Zenty asked how he had spent his morning. Well, he had gone to church with his father, graded papers, and read *Peanuts*. And she? Gone to church, too, of course, and then just sort of pottered about. Actually, though she did not say so to Wig, she had hunted out her old paintings that she had copied from her father's. Surprising how many barn scenes her father had painted. She had a vague notion that he'd had some special reason, but it escaped her at the moment. She had not, to her disappointment, found a copy of the precise painting that hung in the gallery of the Teiler home.

The car swung into a street of wide lawns, beginning to grow green and bright, and stopped before a modified Dutch colonial house, hedged around with boxwood. An herby fragrance drifted on the mist, and she thought how pleasant it would be if she really were coming home. What was it like truly to come home? Would she ever know?

Home to Wig's house and hers . . . maybe? She ought not even to pretend. Yet she did.

Here they were, walking side by side, on the path. And here was spring in the rain—new green leaves on the lilac bushes and patches of crocuses, yellow and white and purple, under a pepperidge tree.

Wig followed her onto the porch that enclosed two sides of the house and reached round her to ring the bell.

"Should have my father's walking stick," he said. "He makes quite a thing of ringing doorbells with it."

"Sometimes I have a notion that you poke fun at your father."

"Who has a better right, eh? Ever think of that?" He smiled down at her, and did she imagine that his eyes slowly, deliberately, took in every detail of her face? She felt again apprehensive. Always she hedged, even to herself, about her attitude toward Mom, but now Zenty admitted that she was—well—hesitant, afraid Mother would embarrass her daughter before Wig. Now father . . . He could be smeared with paint and shadowed with an unshaved beard and yet Zenty never worried about him with any of her friends.

A new maid opened the door and after taking Zenty's and Wig's raincoats led the two young people into the living room where a wood fire blazed cheerfully in the grate. The Kohlmans were generous with their home and always insisted that Mrs. Sperrow entertain her guests downstairs rather than in her own quarters. Zenty was grateful to them, today especially. As Wig walked over to a glass-top table that held a collection of antique guns and studied them, Zenty sat down gingerly on the edge of a charcoal-colored sofa and clasped her hands tightly to hide her nervousness.

Shortly she heard her mother's footsteps and took a deep sustaining breath. Mrs. Sperrow came hurriedly into the room. She stopped upon noticing her guest, exclaimed, "Wig, what a surprise!" and held out both hands to him. Mother always took a somewhat proprietary air toward her ex-patients as if her ministrations had given her a nanny's privileges. "Here, let me look at you." She surveyed him and nodded.

"Pass inspection, do I?" Wig asked.

"Oh, you'll do all right, but you need a scolding, that's what you need. Not visiting us in a coo's age or some kind of age. You'll have to ask Zenty what kind. She knows all the words. Anyway, not since she left me."

So, Zenty thought, it *was* going to be one of those Sundays when Mom jabbed with her offhand remarks—whether intended to annoy or not, Zenty could never be sure. Left Mom, indeed! As if the idea had not been hers that Zenty live with the aunts. However she decided anything, she was wrong. She was always wrong. And maybe she was—scarcely in the house and already fuming. She eyed Mom and Wig morosely.

Mom had released Wig's hands but still contemplated him. She stood tall and handsomely formed in a rich brown dress with a large clip of topaz-colored stones. She wore earrings to match and brown patent leather pumps. Her dark auburn hair waved perfectly back from her squarish face. Her sturdy complexion, unassisted by make-up except for a faint touch of lipstick, had the clean coloring of a young girl.

She turned now to her daughter. "You didn't tell me you were bringing your beau to tea, but then you never do tell me anything."

A smile twitched at Wig's lips, and Zenty blushed, and the knowledge that she was blushing sent the color even more hotly to her face.

"Frankly," Wig said, "I barged in. I can't stay but a few minutes."

"Fiddlesticks," Mom said. "You'll stay to tea now, you hear? A big boy like you can always eat."

"Generally, yes," Wig conceded. He was grinning openly, no longer trying to conceal his amusement.

"So you noticed our gun collection, did you?" Mom asked. "Did you see our silver spoons, too?"

Our guns . . . *our* spoons, Zenty thought. To hear Mom, one would think the house and everything in it belonged to her. But maybe in a way everything did—temporarily. Wherever Mother worked, the moment she stepped in the door, she was a part of the household—a very necessary part—and she shared possession of all the lovely things about her simply because they created an atmosphere for her to enjoy, too. What was more: She had not the worry of caring for them nor even of cooking her own meals. She had only to minister to her patient, and that she did excellently.

It occurred to Zenty then that what Mother had arrived at was a compromise between what she had hoped for from her marriage and what she could otherwise have arranged for herself. For an odd moment, she appeared to Zenty not as "Mother" but simply as a person who had had her dreams and her problems and still did. Then as she led Wig to a corner where another glass-encased table stood beside the sofa, Mrs. Sperrow tapped her daughter lightly on the head, and the gesture dispelled the brief independent image.

Zenty folded her arms tightly and hunched forward to look into the case as Mother pointed out the rows of demitasse spoons—each spoon with a molded handle of different design.

"They're all from abroad," she told Wig, and then with a sly glance at Zenty: *"Abroad? Aboard?* I have to be so careful with my daughter around."

Wig's eyebrows shot up but he continued to gaze at the spoons without looking at Zenty, and Mom pointed out the various handles—a gondola, the Leaning Tower of Pisa, the Eiffel Tower, a fleur-de-lis from Florence, and the Lion of—"of what, Zenty?"

"Lucerne," Wig said.

"You been abroad, Wig?"

"A few times," he said.

"Well, well! Now me—I'd rather see my own country first," she told him, and nodding toward the case, she said, "We use them sometimes."

At the *non sequitur,* Zenty choked back a nervous giggle, and Wig said teasingly, "Do you now?"

Mom eyed him sternly. He grinned at her. And it occurred to Zenty that they were enjoying each other, and just possibly Zenty Sperrow was a mite jealous. She leaned back and tried to relax but almost immediately straightened up again as Mom patted a cherry-red cushion on the sofa and said, "Now, Wig, you sit down while I fetch the tea, and we'll all rest and feast ourselves." In the doorway, she paused, and Zenty waited for the usual admonition.

"You two be good," Mrs. Sperrow said.

Zenty tightened her entwined fingers and wished fervently that Wig would leave.

And so he did—about an hour later after Mother had

fed him pastries and water cress sandwiches and tea with lemon which she said was too *tarty* for her, and she just could not imagine how anyone could drink tea without milk and sugar. At the door, he shook hands with Mrs. Sperrow, took Zenty's icy fingers in his, and snubbed the end of Zenty's nose with them.

As the buoyant sound of his footsteps retreated along the walk, Mrs. Sperrow said, "Well, now, it was nice to see Wig again, but I must say, Zenty, you're no belle of the ball when it comes to entertaining a boy friend. Wig must have thought the cat got your tongue."

"Oh, Mother!" Zenty exclaimed. "I hate that term 'boy friend.'"

"If it isn't one thing you're hating, it's another," Mother said philosophically and, reaching over, tugged playfully at her daughter's hair. "My, I can remember when I'd have given my eye teeth for a handsome beau with money."

Reluctantly Zenty smiled then, but she was worried. Surely Mom did not imagine that Wig was seriously interested in the Sperrows' daughter. She said, scarcely thinking, "The question is, of course—would a handsome beau have wanted you without your eye teeth?"

She never learned. Never. She never could predict what would and what would not offend. Mrs. Sperrow whirled sharply about.

"You think you're funny, don't you?"

"Oh, Mom," Zenty pleaded, "I was only joking."

"Yes, I know your little jokes. I'm terribly funny, I am. I about kill you, I'm so funny. And you spring Wig on me —just like that without telling me—just to see what I'll do. And look at you—in old rubber-sole shoes."

"It was raining," Zenty said defensively. "And besides, I had no idea I'd meet him today."

"Oh, I could shake you," Mother said. She walked over to the tea cart and picking up a few crumbs, nibbled at them thoughtfully. "Maybe now I never mentioned this before," she said, "about when you get married, you know. You needn't worry how you'll pay for the wedding. I'm not rich, goodness knows, but we'll manage a real pretty wedding for you."

"If you can afford a wedding," Zenty said angrily, "why can't you lend me enough for a year at college? Just *one year,*" she begged. "Afterward I'll manage on my own, and I'll pay back every cent. I know you have your future to think of, too."

"Now stop it," her mother commanded. "If you say college once more, I'll scream. Honestly, I don't understand you, Zenty. You got through high school by the skin of your bones."

Usually when Zenty and her mother got into their arguments, Zenty ended up wanting to cry in sheer frustration with herself. This time she giggled instead.

Mother demanded, "What's funny now?"

"Us. You and me. We go round and round, don't we, darling?"

"Yes, we do because you make me mad as a hopper."

"Mad as a *what?*" Zenty started to say and then checked herself. Mom and her malapropisms. If she could not understand her daughter, Zenty thought, neither could daughter understand her mother. Why did she oppose college so vehemently—merely because she did not think it important for a girl? Or because she herself never really liked school and was glad to be through with it? Or because she could not bear to take the money out of the bank? Mom was *very* generous with her time. Of that Zenty always reminded herself. But money? *No.*

"You kids are all alike," Mother said. "Nobody wants to be a clerk or a janitor any more. Nobody wants to work —just keep going to school and going to school."

"School *is* hard work," Zenty said indignantly. "College especially."

"A status symbol," Mom said, for a moment startling her daughter.

"Not for me it isn't," she said. "For me it's like . . . like *food*. Oh, what's the use?"

"You can say that again. Your father has two degrees, and a blessed lot of good they've done him—or me. What have I ever got from him? A bottle of perfume from Paris . . . a straw bag from some island or other. And we were supposed to live on *that?*" She reflected a moment. "And the few hundred dollars he'd bring home once in a cheesy moon."

"Mother, I know," Zenty said, though she knew, too, that the dollars were considerably more than a few hundred—always enough to take care of his child, so Aunt Rhoda maintained. In fact, *she* claimed Mother could have sent Zenty to boarding school all her growing-up years instead of dragging her about from one school district to another before she had time really to make friends anywhere. And if he had not provided for his wife, well, neither had his wife been willing to make a home for him. In the end, Zenty guessed, one believed what one wanted to believe.

"You've managed miraculously, Mom," she said, "and honestly, I am grateful."

"Oh, grateful," her mother said. "You're my baby. I'm not asking you to thank me. I'm just asking you to be fair."

"I try," Zenty said.

"I just wonder if you had to choose between your father and me . . ." She squinted up her eyes as if she were holding back tears. Zenty felt a sudden wrenching pity.

"Can't I love you both?" she asked.

But words were not reassurance enough, as Zenty well knew. Let Father walk in the door and all unthinking she would fly to him with arms open. And in no time she would be chattering to him, telling him all her secrets, laughing at his wit. No, probably she was not fair *except* that her father *listened* to her. He could cut her down sharply sometimes, but always he was willing to let her be *herself,* and Mom was not.

Zenty sighed and said, "I had a card yesterday from Father—from London. He mentioned a 'jolly good showing' but not whether it was his." And then, hoping to mollify her mother, Zenty said, "With Father we certainly do play guessing games, don't we?" She laughed tentatively, but Mrs. Sperrow did not respond. "He also spoke about school. I suppose he means my class with Wig. Do you think?"

Still there was no reply, and Zenty asked, "Did you hear from him, too?"

Mrs. Sperrow hesitated—long enough to betray herself. "Yes," she said shortly, "but I don't know where the letter is now, and I can't go rooting-tooting around upstairs and disturbing everybody."

"Where are the Kohlmans?" Zenty asked.

"Now you know they're out," Mrs. Sperrow said.

"They're always out on Sundays, aren't they? Or practically always, except sometimes the aunt or the old lady. She's sitting with Hory."

"Oh," Zenty said. So who was everybody? And why was Mom so piqued? Could one not even inquire about word from Father without rousing jealousy? Zenty said absently, "I thought I might read to Hory."

"Oh, read, read, read," Mom said. "Hory's resting now and I'd rather you didn't disturb him. Later he can look at television. Oh, my heavens!"

"What?" Zenty asked in alarm.

"The Barrys."

"The who?"

"On Channel Ten. Good gracious, I almost forgot. Run into the den quick and turn on the set, will you? I'll just see as Hory and the old lady are okay and then I'll be right down."

"But isn't this your afternoon off?" Zenty asked.

"Oh, but I couldn't *really* leave Hory with the old lady, you know."

"Mom, you're awfully good to your patients," Zenty said in honest admiration.

On the third step, her mother turned and gazed down at her daughter thoughtfully; then smiled sweetly in a way that always made Zenty somehow ashamed of herself— and regretful, too.

"Thanks, honey," Mrs. Sperrow said. "Now I'll be right down and after we'll have a little supper, and there's a good play on tonight."

"Yes," Zenty said, and as she went on toward the den, she felt again a familiar weight of gloom—of guilt and affection and exasperation all mixed together. But then, maybe Mom felt the same tangle of emotions because of her daughter.

Darn!

You could have wood carvings and etchings on the wall and a fire in the fireplace and the tea cart waiting, and without understanding you had not much of anything at all, had you?

She turned the dial of the television set and watched the screen come to life as she waited. And it was not until hours later when she was walking home in the chill April night that she suddenly guessed why Mom had refused to hunt Father's letter.

In it, Zenty would bet—she would bet anything—he had mentioned a check enclosed for his daughter's support.

SIX

School suspended for Easter week. Three days passed, and she did not see Wig nor did he call. And, of course, she had not expected him to, she told herself. And if she left the house of a morning with one ear tuned still to the telephone, well, ex-high-school friends were home for vacation and were bound to ring her up. And if evenings she lingered outside the clinic a few moments longer than usual . . . well . . .

Well.

When more than half the week had dragged by, she began to count over Wig's faults. In class sometimes, he appeared dictatorial. He had an air of superiority—unconscious, maybe, but there nonetheless. He was altogether too accustomed to wealth. She would bet he had never had to struggle for anything. How would one get on with a man like that? And he *was* seven years older than she. His attentions had always pleased her, naturally, but she supposed that lately to have a mature man interested in her had really flattered her. So now it was her vanity that was hurt by his neglect. That was all, she assured herself.

On Friday, she went to a movie and later to a sweet shop with a boy named Howie Barnard whom she had known at West End High. Zenty had always liked Howie and remembered hilarious times with him. But this night, she watched him in stupefied silence. He talked incessantly—boasted of his freshman antics at college, imitated his professors, dramatized his stories with shouts and growls and gestures. He ducked halfway under the booth table to illustrate how he had hidden from the sophomores in his fraternity. And sometimes in his excitement, he clutched her arm.

Between tales, he ordered the soda fountain clerk around with a make-it-snappy-boy-chop-chop.

Zenty could not decide whether he was trying to impress her, like the proverbial youngster riding bicycle no hands, or whether she had simply outgrown his kind of nonsense. All the while, Wig kept popping in and out of her mind. At one point, she muttered, "Go away," and Howie said, "What?" startled, and she told him she was talking to a fly.

By Saturday—which was her day off—she was thoroughly disgruntled, but not because of Wig, she said. She sat downstairs in the dining room and let herself be annoyed by little things—the dust on the plates that decorated the plate rail just below the ceiling, a thread caught in the filagreed molding above the door, the green glass shade that hung, suspended by a huge chain, above the center of the table. April sunshine winked off the beaded fringe and cast speckles of light on the plastic place mats. This morning the golden oak paneling seemed to close her in. She felt as if she were living inside a tree.

And there she was—talking down her digs again, as Aunt Doris, bless her British murder mysteries, would say. The trouble was, Zenty thought, she did not want digs. Occasionally she had sensed that the aunts were of two minds about housing their niece with them. They did rather need her room and did, she guessed, feel a responsibility for her that rightly belonged to her parents. She did not blame the aunts. But how could she settle in mentally even if she wanted to? Somewhere there ought to be a home. She sat disconsolately absorbed in a lithograph that hung by cords over the sideboard. The picture was not art but had always pleased her because of the Victorian figures—a young couple with four children—that skated on a snowy pond. Down in the margin of the picture appeared a tiny sketch of the same figures in a horse-drawn sleigh. Zenty liked to imagine they were homeward bound to an immense stone house behind the woods that edged the pond. This family was her family and she had concocted endless stories about them all.

The fantasy usually comforted her no matter what the time of year, even in April's softness. But now a remark of her mother's stirred uneasily in Zenty's recollection. If Zenty was so crazy for her own home, then why did the girl "hark" on school all the time? Why did she not settle down with a nice steady boy friend who would *give* her a nice home? And Zenty never could explain satisfactorily why she felt she had to prove herself before marriage— why she believed that only so could she avoid an incompatible mating like that of her parents.

And besides . . .

She shifted her glance from the lithograph to the patterns of light that shimmered across the table and frowned at a sudden realization. Besides, the home she wished for so ardently was a *childhood* home of happy memories. What she wished for had never existed nor ever could.

She traced the edge of the place mat with the handle of her spoon. In a way she was lucky though—maybe luckier than she knew. She could paint away her frustrations. Right now she had an idea for the Teiler contest—a home scene with children grouped in the firelight as they listened to a record player. Already she could visualize the forms, the masses of light and shadow, the balance of colors. And briefly she was excited as absently she watched the aunts—both of them absorbed in the morning paper which they had divided between them.

Their childhood had been something to envy—all sorts of fun in a big old-fashioned house on Long Island. A pony and cart. Weekly trips to the city to lunch with their father and hear children's concerts. Yearly visits upstate with grandparents and rides in swanboats in a place called Seneca Park. Maybe she would write about the aunts' experiences for class.

And maybe she would not. Wig might imagine she was trying to impress him.

Aunt Rhoda glanced up from her paper and said, "You're quiet this morning, chick. Not awake yet?"

"Oh, yes," Zenty said. "Just thinking I've let my homework go, and now I'd better get with it."

"What's the subject this time?"

"I keep changing my mind. Maybe I'll write about the jelly beans."

"Jelly beans!" Aunt Doris exclaimed, coming suddenly alive. "Jelly beans. Things sure have changed since I went to the little red schoolhouse." She rattled her paper and folded it back. "You mean how they're made. I've sometimes wondered myself."

"No," Zenty said with a laugh. Depend on Aunt Doris for the practical approach. "The time I swiped them."

The two sisters exchanged glances. "Hmmmm!" Doris said.

"Remind me to lock up the jelly beans," Rhoda said. "Are you writing for class or *True Confessions?*"

"Oh, now, Aunt Rhoda! I almost always write autobiographical stuff." Suddenly, morosely, Zenty wondered why she revealed her childhood secrets to Wig. How could she be sure he did not think her girlish and silly? But then why care if he did? Doggone him!

"Where did you steal the jelly beans?" Aunt Rhoda asked.

"Just licorice ones—at the nursing home—when the staff had a party and everybody got Easter baskets."

"Were you caught?" Aunt Doris asked. "And spanked, I hope."

"No. That's the twist, see? Uh—no, I wasn't caught, but that same vacation, I played with a new little girl, and we were teasing each other, and I hid her paper doll. And she called me a thief—just jokingly, but, boy, did I kick up a row!"

"So?" Aunt Doris said.

"Oh, Doris," Aunt Rhoda said. "For you we draw pictures. A youngster called Zenty a thief, and Zenty threw a tantrum because she knew she was one. She had swiped jelly beans."

"Oh, is that the pitch?" Aunt Doris asked. "Well, I'm glad she's writing it, not me. Education has certainly changed since I was a girl."

Through the open window came the sound of dogs frisking about the empty parking lot owned by the bottling works next door. Somewhere at the back of the house a vacuum cleaner hummed and in response the canary that belonged to the Pryors' housekeeper began to trill. The slightly burnt smell of warmed-over coffee drifted in from the kitchen.

Suddenly Rhoda exclaimed, "Oh!" as if she had been stung. "Oh, dear! I forgot, Zenty, and I'm sorry. Oh, dear, I do have a head like a sieve. I forgot to tell you your mother called."

"For mercy's sake," Aunt Doris said, "you don't have to eat dirt. What did Molly want?"

"She didn't *want* anything. And for your information, ma'am, I'm talking to my niece, and I'll eat dirt if I please."

Usually the aunts' mild squabbles amused Zenty, but mention of her mother had stirred up again a resentment that had troubled her all week. Mother and her hoarding.

"She's had two dresses laid away for you at the Juniors'," Aunt Rhoda said. "And you're to go there and try them on."

"Two dresses? For me? But I can't afford them. I'm barely recovered from paying for my course this term."

"You don't have to afford them. She's buying them for you."

Zenty blinked. More than ever now she was convinced that Mother had received money from Father, but if Zenty inquired she knew what the answer would be: either that the financial arrangements between her parents were their business—all true enough, she admitted grudgingly —or that the money had been set by for a rainy day which was a euphemism for everything from illness to the as-yet-unneeded trousseau.

"Yes, dear, I know," Aunt Rhoda said. "I was a mite surprised myself." She stopped at a warning scowl from her sister, who never permitted criticism of Mrs. Sperrow.

"The Juniors'?" Zenty said, puzzled. "What is it? And where is it?"

"In a basement, your mother said, on Memorial Square catty-corner to my store."

Zenty shook her head, frowning. And Aunt Doris said, "The . . . Pin . . . Money . . . Shop," in a voice that expressed disgust at the stupidity of her sister and young niece. "Run . . . by . . . the . . . Junior . . . League."

"Ho!" Rhoda said.

Zenty crossed her eyes. "The Juniors!" she said.

"Never you mind, now," Aunt Doris told the girl. "However your mother may abuse the language, she's no-body's fool. She's a good conscientious nurse."

"Who said she wasn't?" Aunt Rhoda demanded. "Lots of good people can't speak the King's English."

"Then stop acting as if malapropisms now and then were a disgrace. Actually they're amusing."

If you're not related to the Mrs. Malaprop, Zenty thought. And Aunt Rhoda said, "Why Doris Sperrow! You as went to Briarcliff Hall. You as were taught that correct speech is part of good manners. You as learned never to offend the ears, the eyes, the nose of others."

"And that's about *all* we learned," Aunt Doris said. "Nothing so mundane as how to make a living—outside gift shops and art stores."

"Ah, yes, work," Aunt Rhoda said cheerfully. She glanced at her wristwatch and folded her half of the paper. Shortly the three women rose, and as Zenty waited for her aunts to precede her, Rhoda whispered, "Shall I go with you to the Juniors'?"

"Oh, would you?"

Aunt Rhoda nodded. "Stop by the store for me about eleven-thirty."

"Yessum."

Zenty watched as her aunts picked up hats and gloves from the hall table and carefully put them on before leaving. After the door closed, she turned toward the stairs, thinking she might block out her painting for the Teiler contest.

She ought to be excited—not just about the painting but about the dresses, too. Yet somehow she was still disgruntled.

SEVEN

The Pin Money Shop was three steps down from the street. Large barred windows on either side of the door let in light from the Square. When Zenty and Aunt Rhoda entered the room, it was empty of customers. A few racks with garments ranged side by side were in the center. Off at one end stood a card table with a few pairs of shoes and a miscellaneous collection of junk jewelry. At another folding table near the right-hand window sat a girl with naturally blonde hair which caught glints of sunlight in a halo across the crown of her head. She was scowling over a book. The place had a dusty smell, and everything, to the soiled red-and-white candy-striped sofa that was presumably for the convenience of customers, was so obviously secondhand that the girl appeared as fresh as a newly minted penny among old coins. Zenty, the artist, appreciated her, and as briefly she studied the girl she had a sense of having seen her before.

Aunt Rhoda said, "Miss," rather sharply for her. She and Aunt Doris both amused Zenty when she shopped with them because, being sales clerks themselves, they had definite ideas about how others in their business should behave. Hastily the girl dropped her pencil and rose.

"Oh, I am sorry. May I help you?"

She was slim, though not thin, and gave the impression of fragility—the delusive sort, Zenty thought, acquired by horseback riding, swimming, ballet dancing, tennis playing. Eyes, direct and blue, regarded Zenty and she realized that the sunny-haired girl, too, was sizing up her compeer as if vaguely remembering other meetings. Suddenly the girl smiled.

"I'll bet you've come for the burnt orange dress," she said.

"Two dresses," Zenty said. "Cassandra Sperrow."

"Yes, yes. I just *knew*."

She darted to the back of the shop and returned shortly with the garments over her arm. She indicated the dingy sofa. Gingerly Zenty sat down beside her aunt while the blonde girl removed the covering from a silk frock of a deep, rich burnt orange. She held the dress under her chin and pulled back the simple classic lines.

"It's not right for me, of course," she said, "but with your coloring . . ."

"It's beautiful," Zenty said.

The girl slid the second garment from the plastic shield and held up a fine, pebbly wool jumper and jacket of forest green with a satin blouse in a dainty, springtime print of lighter greens, soft yellow, pale blue, and occasional squiggles of woodland brown.

Now the girl spoke to Aunt Rhoda. "Don't you think they both look like her?"

Aunt Rhoda nodded, and turning back to Zenty, the girl said, "If I were you I'd match my shoes to these pale blue flecks—maybe in patent leather. Probably you know the trick of matching accessories to a minor color in a print. I didn't until my cousin told me. She haunts designer shops in Paris, and she was the one who sent the orange, but why to me I'll never know."

Zenty listened less to the words than to the effervescence of high spirit and felt suddenly depressed and anxious to get away.

She said, "Have you dressing rooms?"

"Cubbyhole," the girl confided with a laugh and led Zenty to the rear of the huge room and brought a chair for Aunt Rhoda who sat half in and half out of the doorway, bulging a red curtain with her back.

Reluctantly Zenty pulled off her blouse and stepped out

of her skirt. Some day, she promised herself glumly, she would buy one extravagant slip to wear *only* when she shopped for clothes—to impress clerks, especially if by odd chance they happened to be college students as well. Right then, Zenty almost did laugh at herself, but some inner demon persisted in gloom.

When the clerk had fastened the neck of the burnt orange dress, Zenty surveyed her reflection gravely in the mirror. The lush color deepened the duskiness of her hair, made her skin translucent, and the irises around her large dark pupils a clear amber. A loose eyelash troubled her. She blinked, and it fell onto the back of her hand where the lash lay long and curled. She thought childishly that she ought to wish on it—maybe that something tremendously wonderful would happen when she wore the dress for the first time. The fair-haired girl interrupted Zenty's thoughts.

"Oh, lovely!" she murmured. "Can you see how the back fits? You're a perfect size ten."

"Ten!" Zenty exclaimed, and felt Aunt Rhoda's toe surreptitiously touch her in warning, but in warning of what Zenty had no notion.

"And something else, too," the girl said. "This dress has never been worn." Well, that was a blessing not to be overlooked, Zenty thought glumly. "Come outside. Our other mirror has better light."

From the shop proper, a high young voice called, "Nonie!"

"Here," the blonde girl answered, and as she and Zenty edged around Aunt Rhoda and stepped clear of the clothes racks, two young women, probably in their early twenties, turned and stared. Both sported small flowered hats and beautifully tailored suits, and the shorter of the two wore pixie-shaped glasses with gold decorated tips.

"Hmmmm," she said to Nonie, "I see what you mean. It really wasn't for the likes of you, was it?"

With a quick smile, Nonie excused herself to Zenty and walked across to the newcomers where they whispered together over parcels that the girls had brought. Having examined the dress from all angles, Zenty hurried back to Aunt Rhoda.

"Who is that girl?" Zenty whispered.

"Probably a Junior League member who donates her time. Now, look, chick, try the suit on quickly, will you? I must get along, you know, and I thought we'd eat lunch in the park."

Zenty obeyed and was buttoning up the jacket when Nonie returned.

"You're one of the lucky ones," she observed. "Any color suits you."

As Nonie wrapped the new outfits, Zenty slipped into her street clothes; then left the store, aware that the flowerhatted girls watched after her and her shabby blue plaid coat. She wished she *felt* lucky.

The Square was sun-washed, and the air drowsily warm. Pigeons fluttered around the cannon in the center of the park. Women strolled with baby carriages. Two boys who were trying to raise a kite off the ground ran back and forth beside the monument. Spring! And one ought to be grateful just for the sunny weekend, if nothing else. But she could not seem to be grateful for a blessed thing this Saturday.

Aunt Rhoda had brought sandwiches from the delicatessen, and with her niece now crossed the park and found a bench in a shady spot away from the eyes of the Pin Money Shop. Zenty nibbled at her baked ham sandwich, feeling that she ought to eat though she was not really hungry. As a child she had been actually skinny and sometimes worried that she might be again.

"Ten," she said irritably. "How could I possibly wear a size ten?"

Aunt Rhoda swallowed a bite of dill pickle before replying and then said, "The same size would be a twelve in cheaper clothes. When you buy expensive stuff, you get a bit of flattery thrown in."

"They are sort of fancy-dancy castoffs, aren't they?" Zenty agreed.

Aunt Rhoda stooped to pick up a marble from among

the violets. Squinting, she held it to the light. "Oh, not exactly castoffs, honey. Tired-offs. The suit probably wasn't worn more than a half dozen times, and the dress, remember, the girl said hadn't been worn at all. I suspect the color wasn't right for her, and she donated it to the shop."

Aunt Rhoda set the marble back among the spears of grass, and Zenty began to roll it gently to and fro with the toe of her shoe. Hand-me-downs from strangers she had worn most of her life. Once she'd had a terrific fight in school when a patient's daughter had screamed that Zenty had *her* dress on. And so Zenty had. Sometime she would like pretty clothes that were all her own. Now, she supposed, she would glance at every size ten or twelve that bounced down the street and wonder whether the green suit had been hers.

A disgusted whisper in her mind said, "Well, *don't* glance at every size ten or twelve," but Zenty merely frowned and went on worrying the marble with her toe.

Aunt Rhoda mused aloud, "Mignon. Nonie must be her nickname. Mignon Mercedes, the brain surgeon's daughter."

"Oh, is that who she is?" Zenty asked. "I remember her as a little girl. She visited Wig a couple of times when he was laid up."

"I shouldn't be surprised," Aunt Rhoda said. "Yes, I

remember her now. She came into the store the other day and I sold her an oil-and-gouache—a beauty called *Starlight* by Giuseppe Di Costa."

"Giuseppe?" Zenty exclaimed. "Do you know him?"

"Why, of course. Everybody knows Giuseppe. He's far and away the best artist in Mt. St. Clare. I mean he's really good."

Zenty bent down to pick violets as she battled her sudden forlornness. It was then she noticed the plaque on the stone bench.

"Oh, look," she said.

"The bronze? Yes. All the benches around the Square commemorate young men who died in World War II. More than twenty years ago now," Aunt Rhoda said. "Imagine." Her dark eyes grew reflective. "And they were young and took their youth for granted, too, I suppose. Guess youth wouldn't be youth if it didn't. Still . . . on a sunny April day . . ." She gave a short sniffing laugh at herself. "I sound like Doris."

Zenty twisted the stems of the violets in her hands and could think of no comment to break the uncomfortable silence. Then Aunt Rhoda crumpled waxed paper into the brown paper sack and said briskly, "Well, back to the mines. Oh. Oh, I forgot to tell you: The elder Mr. Teiler came into the store this morning, looking tanned and healthy. He had just returned from a cruise in the Caribbean, I heard him say. Made up his mind one midnight and was off the next morning with his son."

She kept her eyes averted, but Zenty had the impression that in a moment her aunt would glance hastily at Zenty to judge the impact of her news. But she did not intend to speak of Wig. He could at the very least have sent a card.

From a ship?

Certainly.

Maybe he had.

Then why hadn't she received it?

"Very affable he was," Aunt Rhoda said of Mr. Teiler, "but if we ever do approach him about a student loan, Zenty, we shall have to be most businesslike. Mind, I still think that once he understands your problem . . ."

"Mmmmm. Hmmmm," Zenty said skeptically. "Did he buy anything at the store this morning?"

"No." Aunt Rhoda laughed then. "But he certainly asked a mint of questions about the young artists here and around about. Who were they? Where did they live? And then he tacked something on the bulletin board."

The violets scattered into Zenty's lap. "A notice maybe?" she asked. "Of what?"

Aunt Rhoda shrugged. "We were busy this morning."

The two women gathered up their belongings and

started to walk toward the store. Zenty needed a tube of alizarin crimson, she claimed, as an excuse to read Mr. Teiler's notice. From time to time, her large, awkward package banged against her legs, but in her excitement she scarcely minded.

Inside, in the dimness of the store, Aunt Rhoda disposed of her gloves, hat, and purse, and brown paper bag that had held the lunch while Zenty nodded to Mr. Cleghorne, the store owner, who was busy with a customer. Then casually she sauntered over to the bulletin board on which students and artists often left notes for each other. There she read the Teiler announcement but learned little more than she had heard from Wig. Besides the thousand dollar prize ("preferably to be used for education"), there were hundred and fifty dollar prizes for second and third best paintings. Age limits for contestants were seventeen to twenty-five, but nothing indicated an exclusion of women.

She stood wishing away time and the suspense of waiting in excitement that intensified until it was almost a pain. She must not hope too much, she cautioned herself, for hope could be cruel, as she had learned the year the Sperrows lived in the country.

A handsome face, close to hers, peered around at her, and she jumped, for she had not heard Giuseppe's approach. Gyps wore sneakers, faded dungarees, and a

Madras shirt, and she thought of Aunt Doris's appraisal of the store's customers: Youths dressed like circus clowns to whom Rhoda played Dutch aunt.

"It is. It is. It is," Giuseppe said, "the princess herself. My day is made."

Zenty laughed aloud and quickly clasped her hand over her mouth, for fear she would attract Aunt Rhoda's attention.

"How are you, gorgeous?" Gyps asked.

"Oh, weathering, thank you."

"Now that's a fine thing to do provided you weather well," Gyps told her. "Did you see Ole Man Teiler's contest announcement? Think I ought to enter?"

She sobered at once with the faintest breath of a sigh. "Did you notice the parenthesis?" she asked. " 'Preferably to be used . . .' "

"Yeah, yeah, yeah," Gyps said. "The old Teiler strings attached. I noticed."

"Would you go back to school—or what? Would you *like* to go back to school?"

"Listen to the gal. Would I like a million dollars? Would I like a world tour? Would I like a vicuña coat— or even, say, ten extra bucks?"

"Okay," Zenty said. "You've made your point."

"Well, you see, eventually I shall have to get my master's, I suppose, *if* I continue to teach."

"Oh, that's right. You teach. Art?"

He nodded.

"Guess I went to school years too early." Suddenly shy, she said quickly, "Well, if a master's is so important to you, why don't you take a fling at the contest?"

"Bless the child, maybe I shall." He was a restless young man, she observed, with an overabundance of nervous energy. He leaned against the bulletin board so that he could face her, and as he talked, he jiggled one foot, tapping his heel against the floor.

"Of course," Zenty said, feeling she ought to be fair and not purposely discouraging. "You could interpret education any way you chose, I suppose. A trip abroad could be educational or just taking a course at Mt. St. Clare."

"Huh?" Gyps said. "Mt. St. Clare? Those jokers I could teach."

Yes, her father had made the same claim. "Well," she said, "even just painting like mad while you used the prize money to pay the rent could be educational."

"Oh, sure, except . . ." He paused, brooding.

"Except," she prompted.

"Well, scuttlebutt has it that Mr. Teiler, now that he has retired, hankers to be patron saint to the arts—or more likely a little coterie of artists who will promote his ideas. Doggone if I want to be anybody's puppet. And I don't want to be everlastingly grateful. Beautiful, you listen to

Uncle Giuseppe. Don't ever expect *any*body to be eternally grateful to you for *any*thing. There's nothing hangs heavier than a debt you can never pay off."

"But a contest," Zenty protested. "If you win fair and square, you're not indebted surely."

"You could be made to feel so. Oh, probably not by Wig. Don't misunderstand me. His father, though, is a horse of another complexion."

"I didn't know horses had complexions," she said. "Gyps, you're terrific."

"Oh, so you've noticed that, too," he said.

"And modest in the bargain. Tell me: Do you know Mr. Teiler?"

Gyps shifted his weight and began to tap with his other foot. "Well, I don't exactly lunch with him at the Flaming Bush Club, you understand," he said, mentioning an exclusive golf club near Mt. St. Clare, "but I have impressions."

"I'm curious to know what you think."

"Well, off the cuff, I'd say he's . . . um . . . snobbish. Let-the-peons-keep-to-themselves attitude. Like most *nouveau riche*. Of course, he'll do anything for Wig—anything, that is, that senior himself approves of whether Wig does or not. Sometimes drives Wig crazy by trying to protect him as if he were still a kid." Gyps ran his fingernail over the wooden frame of the bulletin board. "Frankly, the old boy makes me uncomfortable. Whenever I've met him, I got the notion he expected me to be his son's batman, fag, or whatever the American equivalent is."

"Are there American equivalents?" Zenty asked, not wanting at the moment to sort out all she had heard of the elder Mr. Teiler.

"Plain to see you ain't never been in the Navy, gal—nor lived in a fraternity house."

"Not even a sorority house."

"Can't imagine a sorority turning *you* down," Gyps said. "Anybody ever tell you, honey chile, you've got a voice like a cooin' dove?"

"Oh, Gyps, you embarrass me."

"Oh, now," Gyps protested, "you should never be embarrassed by compliments. Just smile as if nothing could possibly exaggerate your charms and say thank you nicely."

"Thank you nicely."

He laughed and patted her arm. "Got to be running," he told her. "You think maybe I should enter the contest, huh?"

"I think you should do what you want to."

"Yes, well, there's the difficulty, see. There are things I won't do. I will not—repeat—will not paint poster pictures with every last drop of dew on the roses. Not to win a dozen contests."

He pushed the thumbtacks into all the notes on the bulletin board as if they were his responsibility, and having expended that much excess energy, he departed, whistling a refrain from *La Traviata.*

She stood a moment in thought. Her father had dinned at her over and over that nothing was so precious as one's integrity in his work. He never mentioned integrity in marriage, she thought bitterly, but in art, oh yes. One simply did not compromise. Artists learned from each other, sometimes imitated each other, but regardless of the techniques used, the work of the true artist expressed the artist himself. He did not merely paint, he created.

Wig, too, would agree with her father. And always before she had. But now she was not sure that just this once —just this once, mind—she might not paint whatever she thought would win the contest—gardens with every petal sharp and clear and the powder on the butterflies' wings; or at the other extreme, a banged-up garbage can with a dirty white cat pawing at the refuse, or three cubes and four lines. No, she was not sure that she could resist painting whatever was necessary to please. Just this once. Surely the ends justified the means.

Then she remembered something more her father had said, not to her directly, but to his artist friends in one of their many fiery discussions. No man, her father said, sold his soul all at once, but bit by bit—a little here and a little there. To him, Zenty realized since, selling one's soul meant simply painting to please a fickle public regardless of one's own judgment and instincts.

Oh, well, Father had much to say about everything. Even his daughter did not need to heed him all the time.

She paid for her tube of paint, said good-bye to her aunt, and waved to the store owner. Out on the street, Zenty decided to walk despite her bulky package. From time to time, as she strolled past the park, she glanced at the stone benches, seeing now each bronze plaque that had escaped her before. And everything about her seemed suddenly sharpened—the feathery leaves on the sycamore trees, the moving shadows of pigeons as they flew low over the new green grass, the murmurs of the Square—a child's voice, the drone of an airplane overhead, the clumsy rattle of a cart wheeled from the supermarket—and the warm, warm touch of the sun.

In a better mood, Zenty arrived home twenty minutes later to find a note on the hall table. Mr. Teiler had called and would call back about four. She laughed aloud in the empty hall.

No, no, she could not possibly imagine what had ailed her all week.

EIGHT

During that Easter week of Teiler silence, Zenty had decided—quite firmly—never again to accept a last-minute
invitation from Wig. Maybe she did, as her mother
claimed, cut off her nose to "spike" her face. All the same,
Wig need not imagine that the instant he left her, Zenty
sat in a corner, like a rag doll flung carelessly on a chair,
and waited for him to come back and beckon.

She felt cheated of her indignation, therefore, when he
invited her to a buffet supper at the Teilers' a whole week
away. His father, Wig said, was full of his old bounce
again, after the cruise, eager for young folks around him,
and interested in all Wig's friends.

Why? So he could size them up for suitability? The
question, of course, occurred to Cuss Sperrow with the
chip-on-her-shoulder. Zenty silenced her after a while, and

as the days went by grew more and more excited. She hoped Wig or his father would offer to show her the Teiler art collection, but, if not, she would ask to see *The Red Barn*. She *had* to check on the Sperrow sparrow.

Off and on all week she fretted about what to wear; then decided on the burnt orange even though she suspected that any party of Wig's would naturally include Nonie Mercedes and maybe even the two other girls from the Pin Money Shop. And, of course, they would recognize the dress at once. But let them, Zenty decided. Having forewarned herself, she felt she would be able to meet them with poise.

Each night she tried out different hair-dos until Aunt Doris asked Aunt Rhoda which she thought would wear out first—Zenty, her hair, or the comb. But on Saturday, both aunts—rather unusually—commented on how well she looked.

Wig called for her about four, and they drove off in the green car. The day was bright but cold as if spring had fallen asleep and winter were creeping back for another stay. The crowds around the Square moved briskly, trailing shadows, sharp and dark, along the walks. The benches were empty, and only a lone woman stood feeding the pigeons.

Zenty chatted to Wig about his cruise. He was tanned and freshly shaved and barbered and altogether lovable, she thought. And as she rode she was constantly aware that her hands, even through her white gloves, were icy.

Beyond the Square, the streets widened, the houses became larger and farther spaced—with here and there a wooded section where trunks of birches gleamed with a lively whiteness among the more somber trees, and the new leaves formed a fuzzy haze against the cold blue sky.

Past half a long block of wooded land, the car slowed down and then turned in through an open wrought iron gate. Zenty had an impression of evergreens and the glossy leaves of rhododendron and farther ahead, the fat and faintly pink buds of magnolia trees. The car wound around a circular drive and stopped before a huge white house with a red tile roof and chimney pots, a long veranda precisely divided by steps, and stone flower boxes cemented to stone balustrades.

As she left the car and mounted the stairs, she made mental inventory of everything around her, as if seeing it for the first time, and did not mind that Wig was amused.

"I've often wondered," she said, untruthfully since the question had not occurred to her before. "What is the architecture? Federalist? Regency?"

"Mongrel," Wig said with a grin, and unlocked the front door that opened so noiselessly as to be eerie.

The hallway was warm and big. The aunts' room and

hers could be dropped into the space and lost. We-ell, almost. Off at the left, a stairway curved gracefully through a shaft of light that glistened on the parquet floor, brightened the end of an oriental rug, and sparked off the pendulum of a grandfather clock against the wall. And there was—actually in the hall—a fireplace with lighted cannel coal crackling merrily behind a screen. Nothing looked familiar, quite reasonably, since she had not been permitted in the front part of the downstairs as a youngster. Once she had started to explore and been sternly stopped by her mother, who might herself claim possession of the house but never permitted her child to be a nuisance. The restrictions placed on her then made Zenty self-conscious now. Reminding herself that she had been *invited*, for pete's sake, she was a *guest*, did not lessen her uneasy sense of intruding.

Wig helped her remove her coat and left it on a chair with his for a maid to pick up later. Then he steered Zenty around, and took her hand, and as her cold fingers curled in his, a flash of perception crossed his face. The Caribbean sun while bronzing his skin had lightened his hair, and his eyes in contrast seemed more intensely blue than ever. He would always be a distinguished-looking man, she thought, and felt the stir of a sigh which she promptly suppressed.

"Come," he said. "We'll beard the lion together."

He opened a door at the right, and as she stepped into a room of sunshine and firelight and long, filmily curtained windows, a slight woman of about Zenty's mother's age advanced quickly from behind an archway. She had ash blonde hair, a fair skin crinkled about the eyes, and a delicate air that reminded Zenty of someone recently met.

Wig said, "Mrs. Mercedes, this is one of my students, Miss Sperrow." At once Zenty remembered Nonie, who was probably the woman's daughter.

Stolidly Zenty refrained from glancing down at her dress. She had not counted on Mrs. Mercedes at all. Admittedly it was sheer conceit to imagine the woman gave a hoot what Zenty Sperrow wore. Nevertheless, for her the orange took on an incandescent glow that marked her.

Behind her a deep, crisp voice—much like Wig's—said, "Finished, Sally?"

Zenty shifted cautiously and glimpsed a heavy gray shoulder so close to her that her heart gave an awed thud. She dared not move again, though, for fear in her self-consciousness she would trip over her own feet. In her mind, the orange dress grew as bright as a torch.

Mrs. Mercedes said, "Everything's hidden, Lud," and laughed as Wig added quickly, "Not the family silver, Zenty. Mrs. Mercedes has been fixing up a game for us to play." He laid his hand on Zenty's arm.

"Father," Wig said.

"Ah, yes," said Mr. Teiler.

She turned to meet gray eyes that appraised her steadily. Wig said, "Do you remember this young lady?"

Mr. Teiler bowed, not replying at once, and as if challenged against intimidation, her irrepressible mind wondered where he had learned his formal manners. From a Prussian grandfather? Or a star boarder in his mother's boarding house? Or from the movies?

"No," Mr. Teiler said frankly but pleasantly. "Sorry if I should, but I'm afraid I do not."

Wig looked annoyed. "Zenty Sperrow," he said crisply.

"Ah," Mr. Teiler said, as if he still did not remember. "Good of you to come, Miss Sperrow." He turned back to Mrs. Mercedes, and Wig, with lips pressed tightly, led Zenty to a velvet-covered chair by the fire.

Glancing from the grayed mauve of the upholstery to the muted orange of her dress, he said, "Most decorative," and smiled down at her warmly, approvingly. He rarely complimented her on her appearance and now she repeated the words over and over as a foil against Mr. Teiler's snub—if it had been a snub, if she had not once again too quickly taken offense. She sat primly straight and to divert her thoughts considered how her father would enjoy painting her just so. She could imagine him with easel and palette, standing by the floor-length windows. She could imagine his voice bawling out, "Blast all, Zenty, sit *still*."

And so she did, smiling at her fancy.

Voices murmured in the hall, and she did not move except to turn her head as young couples sauntered into the room. Their glances fell upon her, one by one, and there were fragments of silence. Wig brought his friends over, and she met Nonie; a young man named Archer; two Mercedes brothers, Eddie and Derek; and the girls, Muriel and Jocelyn, who had appeared flowerhatted at the Pin Money Shop the week before. Covertly Zenty watched for a swift exchange of glances as the girls recognized her dress, and there were none. And she grew angry with her own stubborn defensiveness.

For a while, everyone chatted and then Mrs. Mercedes called the group around a large tray set on a corner table behind Zenty's chair. Here she had assembled miscellaneous gewgaws—buttons, a cuff link, a snippet of gray satin ribbon, a doll's shoe, a penny, a sprig of artificial violets, and other odds and ends. Duplicates of the trinkets, Mrs. Mercedes said, were hidden in this and a second room beyond the archway—but hidden openly against objects of similar colors. The game was called Camouflage and the intent was to discover as many hiding places as possible within a half hour after Wig gave the signal to start.

As Zenty listened with the others, Eddie, Nonie's older brother—the dark one with the sideburns—wedged himself between Zenty and his sister and rested a hand on the shoulder of each girl. The gesture might have been friendly or even unconscious, but it embarrassed Zenty, for she could not shake off the notion that a pair of steely eyes observed her constantly.

As the group broke up to begin the hunt, Mrs. Mercedes motioned to Wig and together they left the room. Zenty eased quickly away from Eddie and hurried off toward the long windows—not precisely sure herself what she was after. Without Wig's presence, she felt alien. After a moment of indecision, she began to search the curtains, the rug, the table near a sofa. She had just fingered a book when Eddie stepped up behind her and reaching silently around her, shook the cord of a lamp. There within the tassel hung a doll's shoe.

"Eureka!" he exclaimed in Zenty's ear, and circling her with his other arm, wrote "lamp" after the word "shoe" on his list of hidden trinkets. She stood woodenly still and blushing and hoped that Mr. Teiler had gone on into the farther room, out of sight. She debated whether to push Eddie's arm away or try to duck under, but either gesture would call attention to herself.

She said at last curtly, "If you please."

"Oh, sorry," Eddie said innocently, but a moment later he laughed.

She moved swiftly across the room and hovered over the tray, her unassorted thoughts as helter-skelter as the objects under her gaze. Hearing footsteps behind her, she hurried into the second room where card tables sat side by side and in a bay between bookshelves another table with a checkerboard stood ready for play. She imagined herself alone and started when a voice said, "Lots of goodies in here."

Nonie's younger brother, Derek, squatted by a bottom row of books. He straightened up and smiled at Zenty. She distinguished but barely a freshly sprouted line of hair on his upper lip and wondered fleetingly how much joshing he had already taken over his infant mustache.

"Any luck?" he asked.

"Not much."

"Well, open your big baby blue eyes," he said.

"Don't have them with me," she told him and laughed.

"Well, whatever you've got, they're all right," he said and went on fingering the books.

She smiled at him, and relaxing now, began to make discoveries—a penny fastened by Scotch tape to a row of brass-headed tacks that outlined a chair, the duplicate cuff link reposing atop a cloisonné box, a twin length of gray satin ribbon taped to a silver candy dish, a green button pinned to a drapery.

Footsteps vibrated across the thick carpet. A familiar voice spoke from the far end of the room.

"Great ice breaker this game," Giuseppe said to Derek. "By the time you've knocked into everybody six times you're practically friends for life." He spied Zenty then and cried, "Well, *there* you are."

"Why sure," she said, "I knew I was all the time."

"Smarty! I've been looking for you."

Derek munched thoughtfully at his new mustaches and said, "Come see if you can find anything here, will you? My mother always hides *something* on the piano."

Zenty went over and stood with the two young men. Suddenly she laughed aloud. There on an open sheet of music was a tiny crocheted black button glued to a quarter note.

"*Very* ingenious," she said.

A tug at her hair startled her, and Eddie said, "Show me," and stood so closely behind her that in drawing away from him, she bumped against the piano bench.

Gyps frowned.

Derek said lightly, "Watch this guy. He *claims* to be a wolf."

"Maybe the lady likes wolves," Eddie said.

"And maybe she doesn't," Gyps said with warning in his voice.

Ignoring him, Eddie said to Zenty, "Look, baby, if you'll show me what you've found, I'll show you what I've found. And we'll both win."

"The lady," Zenty said, "does not cheat."

"So there!" Derek said to his brother, but Eddie merely smiled and wiggled his eyebrows.

Gyps continued to scowl, and Zenty grew more and

more uneasy. She was about to suggest that they return to the first room when swiftly Eddie reached around her with both arms, shoving her and the bench against the piano, and drummed on the piano keys. The chords crashed in a bellowing discord around her ears.

Above the racket, Eddie shouted, "Let's you and me play duets. I'm sick of this game."

She closed her eyes against a wave of humiliation and wished she could slump to the floor and crawl under the bench. Then a flooding warmth of anger rushed into her face. She jabbed her elbow smartly into Eddie and yanked away so abruptly that she tripped over Derek's feet. Derek caught and steadied her, and Gyps said in a low, wrathy voice to Eddie, "You unmitigated jerk!"

"Aw, keep your toupee on," Eddie said. "She was posing for us so invitingly when we came in that I just wanted to see if the gal was real."

"You wouldn't care to find out whether *I'm* real, would you?" Gyps asked.

"Oh, please," Zenty begged.

Hastily Derek said, "Oh, hey, now wait. Let us not be rash. You mustn't mind this clown. There's one at every party." And turning to Eddie: "If you weren't my brother, I'd sure wonder where *you* grew up."

She stood in utter bewilderment. How had the whole silly fracas started? She had been posing, had she? Well, she supposed she had—sort of—but not to attract attention and certainly not Eddie. She had not even known he was alive at that time. The conceit of him! She bit her tongue to quiet her anger.

She reached out to Gyps and was about to speak when she noticed in the shadow of the archway a ponderous, gray-suited figure. For the third time in that short afternoon, she flushed as if guilty of an indiscretion. And the angrier she became with herself, the more intensely she blushed.

Gyps caught her hand and said, "Come on, let's pan for gold in the next room."

She suppressed the urgency to say, "Gyps, take me home," and went along into the front room. By this time, the group had fanned out, leaving Gyps and Zenty to hunt unhampered. She found a white pencil among cigarettes in a silver holder, a pebble on the marble mantel, a thimble set atop a lidded pewter pot, a brass button tied to a brass poker by the fireplace, a brown feather stuck into the outside weavings of a wicker basket. She searched in silence, aware now and then of voices and sporadic laughter and the occasional *clump* of the coal as it settled in the grate.

Once Mr. Teiler passed by her and stooped to pick up a piece of tissue. Gingerly he carried it to the fire, pulled back the screen, and threw the tissue into the flames where it flared briefly and flew in sparks up the chimney. There was on Mr. Teiler's massive face such a look of fastidious distaste that when he had left, Gyps caught Zenty's glance and grinned.

Then Wig appeared with a silver dinner bell which he held by the clapper. He poked Zenty gently in the ribs with the handle.

"How are you doing?"

She shrugged. "So-so."

"Brief crisis in the kitchen," Wig said. "Didn't mean to desert you."

"All straightened out by the master's voice?"

"All straightened out by a little oil or, as my father says, soft soap." He leaned against the mantel and watched her with obvious pleasure as she went on halfheartedly to search. Suddenly he snapped his arm around and as he studied his watch said, "You're a distraction, young lady. I'm forgetting my job." Another second and he rang for the group.

Zenty moved to the love seat and Derek lowered himself beside her, but the rest sat around on the floor—Nonie and the young man, Archer, with their backs to the velvet chair.

"Exchange papers for scoring," Wig directed with a wink at Zenty. At once there were groans.

"Professors, ugh," Archer said.

"The world's lousy with 'em," Derek grumbled, "even on weekends you can't escape."

Wig raised the back of his hand threateningly, and Gyps said, "Yah! Yah!"

And Zenty wished she could afford to complain about the ubiquitousness of teachers. Hers were all too few. Absently she checked off the hiding places of the various trinkets as Wig disclosed them but sat up instantly alert when he pointed to the sprig of artificial violets on the tray and said, "You all found these, of course, on the back of the fireside chair."

Eddie muttered, "Who could miss?"

And Archer shifted his long legs and said in a puzzled voice, "Well, someone did." He glanced at his paper, then pointed a finger at Zenty. *"You!"* he exclaimed.

She hung her head in chagrin that the girl in the mauve chair had not discovered the hiding place of the violets. She glanced sheepishly at the group through her lashes. Now she *was* acting, and everyone laughed in approval . . .

. . . except Mr. Teiler. He walked about with a heavy, restless tread and peered over shoulders at first one paper and then another until he discovered that Nonie had won.

"Ha!" he exclaimed gleefully. "I knew you would. I told your mother so. I always spot a winner."

She leaned back, her face softly flushed from the heat of the fire, and laughed up at him.

Derek whispered to Zenty as if in apology for his host's

sudden egoistic outburst, "Funny thing about the old boy, he actually does. Wish I knew his secret. Hunch, he says. Always has a hunch about winners."

But she was watching Archer—long-lined like an El Greco painting—as he squinted at one long-fingered hand and slowly opened and closed it. He looked across at her with faint sardonic amusement. And it seemed to her that some indefinable undercurrent permeated the room—perhaps only a moment's embarrassment for Wig that his father should boast before guests.

From down the hall drifted sounds of movement. Then the doors at the far end of the music room opened.

Wig said, "I believe supper's ready."

Archer jumped up and reached for Nonie. She beamed at him as he pulled her—limp and unhelpful—to her feet. She staggered against him, giggling, and he threw his arm around her. Wig claimed Zenty and Gyps both, and they followed the group into the dining room where smorgasbord food was arranged on a long table, and crystal and silver gleamed, and freesia in a huge springtime bouquet of assorted flowers sent subtle breaths of fragrance through the air.

Sometime after supper, Gyps left and the rest, with the exception of the Teilers, settled down at the card tables for bridge. Zenty had hoped they might dance in the hall or in the recreation room if there was one. She had never danced with Wig, and despite records played on the record player, it was clear she was not about to tonight. He and his father alternated between foursome and foursome and walked about and studied the various hands. As sometimes happens, Zenty's cards were incredibly bad with nothing higher than a jack or a ten. Now and then she murmured apologies to Mrs. Mercedes, who had taken Wig's place as Zenty's partner, but she was good-natured and claimed that she never played anything but a social game anyway. Three hearts and did you know that the so-and-so's were off for Europe. That sort of thing.

The time came for the low scorers to shift to the next table. Archer sprang up as Mrs. Mercedes and Zenty approached. Mr. Teiler touched the girl on the arm.

"Come away from this den of iniquity," he said, "and let's see if you can beat me at checkers, eh?"

She was too surprised to speak—merely stood aside as he called to his son to replace Zenty beside Nonie. Then Mr. Teiler guided Zenty to the bay window. He seated her in the chair on which she had found the penny taped to the brass-headed tacks, and sitting down opposite her, nudged each black checker precisely in the center of each square.

"You know checkers, do you?" he asked.

"A little," she said and rubbed her moist palms together.

1 1 3

Actually she was a good player when she chose to concentrate. She had played innumerable games with Mother's patients and their families—and with her father.

Nonie's voice floated across to Zenty, "Don't give him any quarter. He's tough."

"Oh, now, Nonie, my child," Mr. Teiler remonstrated, "when have *you* found me tough?"

Zenty stared out of the window toward the gate where antique carriage lights shone on glossy rhododendron leaves and suddenly she knew what Mr. Teiler wanted for his son: A girl just like the girl who had married dear old dad. A blonde, fragile-appearing creature with beauty and breeding. A daughter of old friends. At the table Zenty had left, the four were chatting away as if suddenly released from the restriction of politeness. Any subject they could discuss now—mutual friends and acquaintances, remembrances, shared jokes—without fear of excluding a newcomer.

All natural enough, and Zenty did not really mind except for Mr. Teiler's satisfied smile. She sat up straight and determined and planned her moves carefully. At odd moments, she studied him—heavy eyebrows, partly grayed, with a large mole disarranging the right one, tanned skin that contrasted with his thick, silvery hair, a face of broad contours, and a large, straight nose. Just his bigness was an advantage to him, she thought.

She was contemplating a play when he said, "Where do you live now, Miss Sperrow?"

She waited until she had finished her move before replying. "On Elm Street with my aunts."

"Ah, yes," he said, "Carriage Park. I remember that whole section—beautiful once, long before you were born, of course. Where on Elm are your aunts?"

She told him.

His glance roved over the board while he rubbed his forehead with heavy, blunt fingers. After several moments, he said, "Hmmmm," and slid a black checker forward. "Eleven Twenty-Nine, eh? But isn't that the old Pryor place?"

"Yes, sir."

"You are living with the Pryors?" he asked in surprise.

"We have a sort-of apartment."

He shook his head. "Pity how the old houses run down," he said.

Between his evident nostalgia and the occasional bursts of laughter from the bridge tables, she began to feel stranded again. The wallflower at the party. A song from one of Broadway's most famous musicals that spoke of dancing all night drifted hauntingly through the room. She looked off toward Wig, but he sat with his back to her and from the expression on Nonie's face, he was teasing Nonie as she played out a hand. Zenty turned again to the board and just in time checked herself from making a move her opponent obviously expected of her.

"Odd, isn't it?" Mr. Teiler said, "that I was thinking about Carriage Park only the other day and trying to figure out how those lovely old houses came to be abandoned. And, you know, I made an amazing . . ." He stopped abruptly as she pushed a red checker into a square where he was obliged to jump her man. ". . . discovery," he finished.

When she then took two of his men, he said, "Hmmmm."

For endless moments, he was silent as he concentrated on his next move. Gazing steadily at her then, he said, "So you play a little, eh?"

She could not quite repress her smile. "Yes, sir."

"Hmmmm."

She looked over the board, trying to anticipate him, and at once he began to talk again as she slid her tongue over her dry mouth to moisten it.

"Yes, a really interesting discovery," he said, going back to the subject of Carriage Park. "I recalled the first four houses that were sold, and in each case, the owners—how shall I say?—married outside their milieu."

Her fingers tightened on the captured black checker she had been toying with as she studied the board. She set the black checker down, shoved a red one into the front row of her opponent's territory, and said, "Will you crown my man, please?"

He complied, almost absently. "Perhaps I don't mean milieu exactly, but outside the group of old and rooted families." He jerked a linen handkerchief from his pocket and dabbed at his upper lip, and his hand shook slightly.

He had been ill, she recalled, and it occurred to her with a bit of a shock that he was likely a generation older than *her* father. Somewhere she had heard—probably from Aunt Rhoda—that Mr. Teiler had married in his mid-forties a woman less than half his age. Strange world . . . the young Mrs. Teiler gone and the old Mr. Teiler still alive and nostalgic over houses that had fallen to the wrecking crews.

"Sociologically an interesting fact," Mr. Teiler said. "You can trace what happens when rootless families marry into the old established ones. Restlessness infects them all."

He gazed off into the darkness beyond the window and she saw his sharp, brooding profile reflected in the pane. And oddly, for no reason she could name, she was sorry for him. One was not likely to think of Ludwig Hellman Teiler II as a lonely man. Yet he might be, might he not?

Then he said, "Women set the tone in marriage, and men let them. I've never quite known why." Abruptly her pity vanished, and for the first time, she sensed the drift of his conversation, monologue actually. Hands off my son. Or was she being Cuss Sperrow again, touchy and suspicious? Maybe. But she could not repress a slow, mounting anger. He went on talking about his gardens—vegetable, herb, flower—but she did not trouble to listen attentively. All her energy she bent on the game. And after she had startled him with several shrewd moves, he, too, fell silent.

The bridge players had tallied their scores and were lounging about, idly talking, before the last red king had cornered the last black king and Mr. Teiler said, "Congratulations."

By then the palms of her hands were wet. But now that she was victor, she reproached herself. She had really been trying to impress him, but there were men who could not bear to lose. And he might easily be one. Ludwig Teiler II might not forgive nor forget even the loss of a paltry game of checkers. Not soon anyway.

"You were kind to let me win," she said.

He shook his head at her. "My dear young lady," he said, "I have never deliberately let anyone win—not even my son when he was a boy."

Fortunately, Wig walked over before she could think of a suitable comment—if there was one—and said, "Some of our guests are leaving, Father."

"Ah, yes." Mr. Teiler nodded to her and rose.

As Wig pulled back her chair, the penny with the

Scotch tape still attached plopped into her lap. She picked up the coin and laid it on the checkerboard.

"No, no," Wig said. "Here." He peeled off the tape and thrust the coin into her hands. "A penny's for luck. Don't give your good luck away."

She'd need more than the luck of a penny now, she thought, and depressed at her own stupidity went along to bid Wig's guests good-bye.

NINE

The Mercedeses were last to leave, and when they had gone, Mr. Teiler disappeared into his study. Wig left her alone a moment in the hall where the grandfather clock ticked with relentless solemnity. The fire in the grate had long since burned down, and only a few smoldering coals, covered with ash, remained. These remnants of a merry blaze depressed her with a let-down sense of the party-over-and-done. Not just her encounter with Mr. Teiler disturbed her, but some other disappointment stirred at the back of her mind. Then she remembered. The barn painting.

She debated now whether she dared ask to see it. She wound the fingers of her white gloves together, then held the gloves by the middle finger and watched them untwine. Her mother said Zenty was careless of her clothes.

Zenty did not think so—did not think she really was—but occasionally she had to rebel against the reverence for things. And anyway, the gloves were already soiled. And anyway, Zenty told herself, I am what I am what I am, and felt further depressed. And she was not even sure that finding her father's sparrow on *The Red Barn* would cheer her. But she had to see it.

When Wig appeared, looking in spite of his slimness and air of good taste as if he had borrowed some of his father's largeness, she stammered over her request while he watched her quizzically.

Then he said, "Oh, the painting. Of course. Where did my father go? He'd like nothing better than—"

"Oh, no!" she said—too hurriedly—and at Wig's shrewd glance added, "Your father's tired."

Wig did not comment further, but pulled out his key case and selected a small key. "Up the stairs here," he said. "You don't mind walking two flights?"

"How else should we get there?"

"By the elevator round at the back. We installed it right after Father retired."

She had been about to say, "What luxury," but now refrained. As the two climbed the winding stairway, she told him, "I feel like a conspirator."

"For pete's sake, why?"

"Oh, I don't know. We're so quiet—sort of stealthy."

"Zenty pretending?"

"No-o," she said so soberly that he stopped a moment on the second landing and turned to look at her.

"Is something troubling you, Zenty?" he asked.

She shook her head. Nothing except . . . everything. And he was probably right about the pretense. Of course, if the painting did turn out to be her father's, the discovery would eventually enhance his prestige and would certainly vindicate her childish boasting to the Teilers. She might even be tempted to gloat. But her dreams of college or art school in the fall could still remain just dreams. Nevertheless, she told herself defiantly, nothing ever happened without first the dream.

On the third floor, a night light burned. Wig unlocked the nearest door, reached inside, and switched on fluorescent wall lamps that flickered to brightness. A long room sprang out of the darkness, and straight ahead on the opposite wall hung *The Red Barn*.

She walked swiftly around a low green-cushioned seat, vaguely aware that a row of such backless benches divided the width of the gallery, and stood hesitant as one does with an unopened telegram that might contain good or bad news. There was the barn, delicately conceived and yet suggesting sturdiness. There was the creek, bubbling in at the right. There were the autumn greens so often reminiscent, too, of spring. She fought against a welling nostalgia for her thirteenth year—the first of it when she had been excited and brimming with hope—and went forward and scanned the painting eagerly.

And there, yes, there! Barely perceptible under the fallen leaves was the outline of a half-hidden sparrow, but even without the Sperrow signature she would have recognized her father's ambidextrous strokes—a few that he always threw into his paintings. She could see him now, his shirt sleeves rolled back, his old shirt worn outside his trousers, the light shining on the heavy golden hairs on his arms, a brush in each hand as he painted a single stroke with both simultaneously. A bit of unnecessary showmanship, but Father . . .

Hang it all! She was suddenly, poignantly homesick for him. She stood blinking rapidly, and pulling a tissue from her pocket blew her nose softly. She had almost forgotten that she was not alone when she heard Wig's voice, and then it was the note of embarrassment that aroused her.

"Ah, Father!" Wig said, too heartily. "We thought you were resting."

"I'm sure you did," Mr. Teiler said dryly.

Wig flushed and then said with a touch of asperity, "Otherwise I should have asked you to show Miss Sperrow *The Red Barn*. She's been interested in it for some time."

"Has she?" Mr. Teiler said.

Zenty looked at them helplessly, aware now that as far

as Mr. Teiler was concerned she had been an intruder from the start.

"I asked to see the painting," she explained, "because I thought it might be my father's." She paused at the expression—both knowing and skeptical—on Mr. Teiler's face. "And it is," she finished defiantly.

Wig contemplated the toe of his shoe. And she thought, well, darn him—both of them! She felt again a familiar helplessness against their disbelief—a sense of defensiveness that belonged to the days when she and Mother had stayed briefly in this household.

"I can show you," Zenty said. "Look!" But Mr. Teiler spoke simultaneously.

"You might suggest to your father," he said sarcastically, "that he drop in to see me."

"He's in London right now," she told him. She turned back toward the painting, intending to outline for him her father's signature.

"*Is* he?" Mr. Teiler said.

Wig sat down on one of the benches, folded his arms, and stared straight ahead of him. He used to tease her out of her boasting and her fantasies that were no doubt scarcely distinguishable from lies. But she was a big girl now and an embarrassment before his father. . . . Is Zenty playing a game? Apparently Wig still thought so. Very well, let him.

Mr. Teiler said, "Pity your father's away. When you write him, you might tell him I may possibly have a commission for him."

Wig raised his head and glared at his father but avoided Zenty's eyes. Mr. Teiler was baiting her, and for dignity's sake she knew she ought to say her good-byes right then and stop him. But she could not go away unvindicated, and besides, she was curious.

"A commission?" she asked warily.

Wig sighed loudly as if to warn her, but she ignored him. Mr. Teiler jerked a thumb toward the painting.

"I should like a companion piece to this one," he said, "with a springtime setting."

"The same barn?" she asked, for now an idea was floating about nebulously in her mind.

He sucked in his lips as if to hide a smile. "Same barn but slightly different view."

"From the rear of the barn," she persisted, "or the front, showing more of the door, maybe?" Wig stood up impatiently as if about to interfere, and she took a satisfaction now in annoying him—both of them, for their smugness.

"Ummm . . . yes . . . more of the door I should think." Mr. Teiler rubbed his hand across the lower part of his face and pinched the end of his nose between thumb and forefinger.

"The barn in spring," she repeated musingly.

1 2 5

He nodded with exaggerated solemnity. "You started to point out something to me, didn't you, when I interrupted?"

She bit the inside of her cheek as she debated, for she had a sort of plan now, vaguely conceived, and a sense of warning, moreover, to caution. After a moment, she said with a laugh, "Only my father's brush strokes which, naturally, you have already noticed."

She turned to Wig, who was studying a portrait of a child with a teddy bear as if he had never seen the picture before.

"Thanks, Wig," she said curtly. Deliberately she surveyed the row of benches along the center of the room— each cushioned in a different color, each color chosen from a painting. In the exact patches of brightness, the precise arrangement of benches and paintings, and the coolness of the fluorescent lights there was an air of cold perfectionism.

Then Mr. Teiler either remembered that he was still the host or else was impressed by her spunk, for he said, almost apologetically, "Pity Wig didn't think to show you the gallery earlier. These," with a wave of his arm, "are all from my ramblings. The old masters from the Reid collection—my wife was a Reid—are in the next room, but you can't do them justice even in a half hour, you know."

"Thank you all the same," she said and started toward the door.

Mr. Teiler followed. "Wig, will you lock up?" he asked.

They walked along the upper hall in silence. At the top of the stairs, he took her arm and said, "Careful here." As they headed down, he said, "You work at the clinic?" and without waiting for her answer mentioned several of the physicians. Did she know them?

By voice, she told him. Since the switchboard was enclosed in a separate room, she rarely met the personnel.

"And you *enjoy* your work?" he inquired.

"It's a job," she replied.

"Well, yes, I suppose it is." They turned the corner on the second floor and again he touched her arm as they began the descent. "I ask," he told her, "because all evening you have reminded me of someone I could not place."

Myself, she thought—the curious little kid who was forever exploring the back of the house when she was not playing authors or jackstraws or mumblety-peg on a cork board with Wig in his room. Even then he had pampered her, found her amusing because of her tall tales.

"But now I remember," Mr. Teiler said. "The airline stewardess on our flight from Miami. Have you ever considered the airlines, Miss Sperrow?"

"For what?" she asked, startled.

"Employment," he said. "Of course, I have no right to meddle in your affairs, but to see youngsters in misfit jobs always troubles me. I stayed in one overlong myself." He delved into an inside pocket and pulled out a small notebook. "Suppose I call around on Monday and make an appointment or two for you."

"But I—I can't imagine myself an airline hostess," she protested.

"You haven't tried," he said with a smile as he jotted down a reminder. "If I were young again, *I* should be tempted by the travel and the excitement and the youthfulness of the staff. There's a marvelous vigor about the whole business."

She backed away and stood with her hands touching the newel post as if to steady herself against the pull of his influence . . . even more, of the vision he had conjured up of a vast world and holidays in which to paint it. Overhead footsteps sounded and silently she urged Wig to hurry.

"You are precisely the type of young lady the lines are looking for," Mr. Teiler told her.

But she was not a *type*. "I'm not interested, Mr. Teiler," she said. "Thank you, but I'm not."

"Now, now, don't be hasty," he admonished. "I'll phone you. Where? Can you talk freely at the clinic? Or had I better call you at home?"

"Please don't trouble."

"No, I shan't trouble," he promised affably. "Your aunts, I presume, have a telephone?"

"Mr. Teiler," she said, "I can't change jobs now. I'm taking a college course and intend to finish it."

"Yes, well. I shall explain that you won't be able to start until the end of the school year."

She let her breath out softly, repressing her exasperation.

"Please," she said, "before you make inquiries, let me talk to my aunts and my mother."

"Ah," he said, pinching his lower lip thoughtfully. "Yes, I suppose . . . I suppose you ought to. Well, do. And when school is over, I'll remind you again. You shouldn't have the slightest difficulty, you know. The marriage rate among stewardesses is high, I understand, and the lines are always looking for replacements . . . and, of course, many of the large companies have their own private planes. Between us, Wig and I can surely find you a spot."

So Grandfather Teiler and Uncle Wig would look after little Zenty, would they? she thought angrily, deliberately stirring up her anger to mask an overwhelming gloom. Wig thudded rapidly down the steps and ignoring his father said brusquely to Zenty, "Ready?"

She nodded and bade Mr. Teiler good night. He was

tucking his notebook back into his pocket with a fumbling motion that reminded her again of his age. Perhaps Wig noticed and perhaps what he said was intended as a half-grudged olive branch to his father: "I shan't be long." But they were not the words of a man on a date, and she was again the cute little Sperrow youngster being taken home from the zoo except that the zoo had always been fun—with peanuts for the elephants and a balloon for her. She headed for the door, and Wig strode past, and opened it for her.

Outside, the night was chill, and she shivered in her thin spring coat as they walked along the drive. He settled her in the car and slid in on the other side. And they rode silently away from the curb, through the open wrought iron gate, and along the empty streets. Once he seemed about to speak but apparently changed his mind, and she commented then on the success of the party, and he said, yes, he guessed everyone had had a good time. And they were quiet again.

The car passed the Square and turned into Carriage Park. Down Elm Street, ahead of the bottling works, the street light shone on the blistered picket fence and the first leaves of the lilac bush in the corner. Wig stopped the car before Eleven Twenty-Nine, hopped out, and helped her onto the curb. Together they mounted the steps to the porch. As he unlocked the door with her key, she told him again how much she had enjoyed the party. He smiled faintly as he reached in and flicked on the hall light.

He looked down at her and said, "Sometimes I forget how young you are." That was all he said, and then he was gone. And now that she was sure he would not kiss her, she wished yearningly that he had. She stood alone in the hall—bewildered by the emotions of the day that she had not yet sorted out. If her father were home, she could confide in him, and he would talk sense to her. He might even consent to paint another barn picture for Mr. Teiler. Only, no, not Arnold Sperrow. He took orders from no one on what he should or should not paint. And once he finished a painting, he forgot it. He never had had much pride of achievement. Or else he was always too interested in his current project to think about what he had already accomplished.

She sighed, and reaching into her pocket felt the penny that had tumbled into her lap at the Teilers'. She held the coin on her palm in the light. Her lucky penny, hah! She returned it to her pocket and tiptoed upstairs and past the aunts' door. Doris called out, "Zenty?"

At the sound of the familiar voice, tears threatened. But what was there to cry about, for pete's sake? She swallowed against the tightness of her throat, and stepped into the bedroom crowded with heavy furniture that had once been in the aunts' Long Island home and still belonged in a house. The aunts sat propped up in twin spool beds—Rhoda with fat pink hair curlers all over her head and her brown eyes large and questioning. She looked like a child who had grown up before her time. Aunt Doris, on the other hand, appeared severe with her hair pulled tightly under a net cap and her face shiny with cold cream.

They were both so normal . . . so usual . . . this might be any night, but somehow it was not.

Aunt Doris closed her murder mystery over her thumb to hold her place. "Well," she asked, "did you enjoy yourself?"

Zenty swallowed again before she trusted her voice. "A six-layer cake with icing this thick," she said, indicating a half inch with her fingers. Then noticing that they were unsteady, she ran her hand through her hair and fiddled with her purse. Doris smiled, but Rhoda looked troubled.

"What did you do?" she asked.

"Oh." Zenty drew in a deep breath. "Played games."

"So," Aunt Doris said, opening her book again, "you had a pleasant evening, and all your nervousness was for nothing."

"I—I did get overexcited, I guess," Zenty told her aunt. "I have sort of a headache now."

"You never learn, do you, spook?" Aunt Doris said. "Well, there are aspirin in the bathroom cabinet."

"Yes, well, I think I'll go right to bed."

Aunt Rhoda reached up and drew Zenty toward her. She rested her forehead on Rhoda's shoulder that smelled muskily of after-bath talcum powder. But she could not control her tears against sympathy for long. She pulled gently away from her aunt's grip, kissed Rhoda quickly, and said a husky good night.

As Zenty was closing the door, she heard Rhoda say, "She's upset. Something happened."

And Doris, already engrossed in her story, replied absently, "Don't be a donkey."

With eyes smarting, Zenty ran the few steps to her own door, pushed it open, and began hastily to undress. She flung her clothes in a heap on a chair and raced into the bathroom that she shared with the aunts and turned on the shower. Once under the rush of the water, she no longer fought back the tears though she told herself she was silly. What was there to cry about now more than there had ever been? She ought to be happy because of the Sperrow sparrow, and she had not even thought to tell the aunts. All this poor-me stuff. What ailed her?

At length the hot water began to cool. She turned it off and with the towel to her mouth drew in a long gasping breath. "There!" she said. But even after she had climbed into bed, her throat still ached as if she had not exhausted her tears. And why? Because a creep named

Eddie had implied that she was a phony. And suddenly Wig had found her embarrassingly young. And Mr. Teiler had managed to convey without actually saying so his belief that she was not suitable for his son.

The pigeonholers! Doggone them! She kicked viciously at the bedclothes. Doggone *all* pigeonholers! Well, if she had to be labeled, she intended the label to read *artist* in BIG letters.

The sudden flare of anger subsided as she began to fold tucks in her pajama legs and considered the plan that had occurred to her in the Teiler gallery. Sometimes ends did justify means. She had made up her mind—exactly when in the past hours, she could not pinpoint—but she had come to a decision. She would win Mr. Teiler's ratty old contest. And she knew how. She knew now precisely how.

TEN

She roused the next morning when the world was still murky with predawn light. She was always an early riser who never used an alarm, but today she stirred only partly awake with a sense of struggling still to stay asleep, fighting the same heaviness that had troubled her when she knew her parents were about to separate once more. The acrid smell of smoke from burning refuse drifted into the room from an incinerator somewhere along the street and insistently roused her. She jumped out of bed, padded into the bathroom, and running the cold water very slowly so as not to disturb the aunts, bathed her eyes. Thankfully she did not have to visit Mother today. Friends had invited her out for the afternoon and evening. Sometime her mother would have to hear about the Teiler party, but not today. No, indeed. This Sunday, Zenty meant to spend in the country, painting. Mr. Teiler wanted the red barn with a springtime landscape, did he? Well, he should have his painting by an artist named Cass Uhlman. That stupid middle name of hers might come in handy yet.

She dressed quickly, pulled on her plaid kilts and a pale blue sweater, hunted through her copies of her father's barn pictures, chose one, and packed it with her artist's kit. Once again, she puzzled over why Father had painted so many barn scenes, but the reason still eluded her, and she hurried down to the kitchen. There she fixed a sandwich and made an eggnog which she drank as she ate cereal. The breakfast was not the most satisfactory, especially for a Sunday, but would do. Out in the hall, she left a note for the aunts, and as she closed the front door behind her, the housekeeper's alarm clock sent out a wobbly clamor.

Down the street, outside the delicatessen store, two boys were spreading out plastic covers to protect their piles of Sunday papers from the dirt of the walks. The breeze was brisk, and the boys laughed at each other as they struggled to hold the covers while they stacked the papers. She watched the youngsters as she waited for the bus and wondered whether they were always cheerful or whether they were sometimes as restless as she. Ambitious to be doctor, lawyer, engineer, or the best baseball pitcher in the world. What would happen if she walked up to them and told them to go on dreaming, never to stop? They would stare at her and think her crazy and not guess that she was talking to Zenty Sperrow and answering the Teilers.

She boarded the bus a few moments later and settled back into a seat halfway toward the back. Early sunlight showed up the dust on the windows, but whenever the bus passed through the shade she looked out onto the empty streets where occasionally a churchgoer hurried along, missal in hand. Farther on, a man was soaping his car. Right now, she thought, the world belonged to her and the boys with the papers and the bus driver and the churchgoers and the man with the soapy sponge. At the next stop, other passengers climbed aboard, and they, too, shared ownership of the world. But it was big. She loved the bigness of the world in the early morning.

At the outskirts of Mt. St. Clare, the bus dipped through wooded areas where the sun flickered behind the trees. She was now relaxed, as if her tears of last night had refreshed her, and she watched the landscape contentedly. She saw the new curled fern that grew along the road, the ditch with last year's soggy leaves, a stream sparkling over stones, crossroads with signs that pointed everywhere—to Maple Ridge, Straw Market, Purple Hills, East Anglia, and other places she had not time to read before the bus shot by and passed a farmyard where robins hopped in the garden. Now the world belonged to the robins, too, and the world spread farther and farther until it was no longer bounded by Carriage Park or switchboards or Teilers either. Not even they could overshadow the promise of spring on an early Sabbath morning.

Sometime later, she alighted at Green Meadows before a drugstore across from a church. Zenty had been brought up to no formal religion. Her paternal grandfather had been a free-thinker and had refused to let his children affiliate with any sect. Her mother always spoke of herself as a Methodist but rarely attended services because of her patients. Sometime in Zenty's thirteenth year, though, Zenty had decided that churchgoing was a part of orderly family life and had rarely missed a Sunday since, trying first one church and then another. She crossed the street now, mounted the steps, and found a dark corner of the vestibule where she could leave her kit. Then she went into the church proper, and the moment her mind was still, anger with Mr. Teiler returned, and she had constantly to pull her thoughts away and concentrate on her prayers.

She could not decide precisely when she spotted Giuseppe Di Costa. He sat several pews away so that she saw only the back of his head at first, but someone—his mother, perhaps—began to sneeze, and as he turned to look at her, Zenty recognized him. When the service was over, the Di Costas left by a side door and by the time she had retrieved her kit and reached the street, Giuseppe was nowhere to be seen. Near the church, she boarded another bus for Wood Hollow Road, and all the way she thought about Gyps. No wonder he had looked familiar to her the first time they had met. She had probably passed him often on the streets of Green Meadows when she was a skinny youngster with a head full of dreams.

It was still early—not yet eight-thirty—when she alighted. She took in deep breaths of the morning air— fresh and still cool—and then began the trek along Wood Hollow Road. In a barn, a boy was milking a cow. Farther on, in a driveway, a man was lifting a sulky-faced child into a car beside her brothers and sisters. Zenty slowed down so as to watch the family and wondered whether she, too, might have balked at times if she had lived in one house all her life and been subject to routine. Would she have rebelled? Would she have cried for change? Was she not crying for change now? Although, it seemed to her that her restlessness was not just boredom, but a searching for her place. And she was afraid that fate would decree the switchboard and Carriage Park to be Zenty's place. And she could not bear to have her world—either of thought or things—so limited.

She sauntered on, and as she passed the familiar wooded strip became aware that her heart was pounding with excitement. She rounded a bend in the road and stopped in shock at sight of the house. It had stood empty since the Sperrows had left, but she was not prepared for the despoilment of the few years between. Windows were broken—sills rotted. One corner of the porch had collapsed. It was under the porch that Mom had discovered a snake—a harmless one, Father had said. But harmless or no, Mom had declared, she was through. And Father had said he did not understand how she could be through with what she had never started. And Mom had demanded to know what he meant. And Father had told her she could not be through trying to make a home when she had never begun—when from the first day she had been looking for just such an excuse to move out. So they had argued—Father bitter and sarcastic, and Mother always at a disadvantage because she could not express herself nearly so well and sounded more ridiculous the angrier she got. Her parents, Zenty realized now, were miserable that day. Then she had supposed only she was. Her world had crashed, and though she had known a long time before that it would, she had hoped it would not.

She had been so eager and full of plans when the Sperrows moved to Wood Hollow Road. She remembered finding an old sewing machine and some blue-green draperies in the attic. Her father had oiled the machine and helped her to fit the material to make a cover for the couch in the living room. Later, as she and Father had cleared out the barn, she had uncovered a can of red paint, and together they had painted the front and back doors of the house. They did look odd but sort of cheery, too, with the rest of the place shabby.

Zenty set down her artist's kit and flexed her arm. "I ought not to have come back," she told herself. Still, here she was. She picked her way along the crumbling walk to the rear door. It was unlocked but warped, and she had to push against it. When the door gave way under pressure, she stumbled into the hall still clinging to the knob. She heard a scampering down in the cellar. Field mice or rats. She hesitated, but then moved on into the kitchen. It was barer than she could ever have imagined. An oblong, lighter than the rest of the peeling paint, marked the place where the refrigerator had stood, and beyond, an end of pipe thrust out for connection to the stove that was also gone. Rust stained the sink, and the linoleum gaped with bulging cracks.

She stood biting her thumb as she debated whether to go on into the rest of the house when she noticed a small black notebook lying under the window. She started across the room, caught her toe, and for a giddy instant struggled against falling, then landed with a crash. She untangled herself and sat back, shaken, and as she rubbed her knees, she thought how foolish she was to risk the floors. If she had broken a leg, whoever would find her here? She retrieved the notebook and stepped out into the hall.

In the silence, the old house creaked, a spider dangled from a thread in the cellar entranceway, and below her the scampering feet made their rustling noises. Oddly, it was her mother of whom Zenty thought then and was glad Mother could not see the place now. For though she hated housework, Mother had scrubbed and polished with a diligence intended, Zenty believed, to offset Mother's lack of enthusiasm. Once when Zenty had neglected to dust the picture frames, Mother had said, "You're lucky. If you'd been raised by my grandmother, she'd have slapped your face with the dirty dust rag." And for a moment, Mother's eyes were bright and hard as if she were still holding back tears because of an old humiliation.

Zenty had not thought then, but she did now as she picked up her kit, that Mother had had her problems in childhood, too. Father was only partly right. Mother had at least kept house and clothes clean and family fed. True, she had not Father's endless patience to strive—to collect furniture piece by piece, to build one cupboard now and another later, to plant a corner of the garden this year and more next. She could too easily walk into a home already established and earn her living there.

Something else had not occurred to Zenty before either —that Mother might have been lonesome for *her* kind of friends who enjoyed bingo and movies and soap opera and neighborhood gossip. Father's friends had come often that year and had sat around in the barn till all hours of the night. Mother never understood that they brought him students and kept him stimulated to paint his best. Constantly she had nagged him about the amount of coffee his friends drank, and Father claimed that if he were a millionaire, she would still begrudge every penny spent.

Oh, where was the right and where the wrong?

Zenty pushed open the door and stepped into the sunshine. Around at the north of the house, she looked for the lilies-of-the-valley that had so excited her when she had first discovered them, and she found them again, choked in damp leaves but pushing through. For the next half hour, she cleaned away the rubbish. She would not return when the flowers bloomed—maybe not ever—but somehow she felt better when she had given them room to breathe and grow.

Finished with her gardening, she ran down to the creek and washed her hands and then carried her kit across the yard to the barn. Yes, it had the well-proportioned lines she remembered. In fact, Father had planned some day to buy the property and remodel the barn for living quarters. How he had loved it, as Zenty had, too.

She walked up to the door and tried to slide it back, but it would not budge. She yanked and she pushed, but snow, rain, heat, and cold had contrived to warp the barn door beyond her strength to move it. Suddenly she was relieved not to see within to the emptiness. She dusted her hands on her stockings—a gesture that had always annoyed her parents and that sometimes she had repeated deliberately to attract their attention. Kids were funny.

She turned her back on the barn and riffled through the pages of the notebook, smiling at her father's small dashing writing. Grocery lists with the inevitable coffee, regular grind; art supplies; notes on students.

"Too stiff," she read. "Needs to loosen up; suggest finger painting."

"Colors muddy; overmixing; demonstrate again."

At the third notation, she laughed softly. It was so like Father. "Imitative; remind class *again* that true artist is independent soul who obeys only his own inner stirrings." How often had she heard *that* theme? Suddenly she frowned and bit her lip as she read, "Suspect cheating, but, if so, how? If so, OUT."

She flipped the page quickly then and the book—slippery from the warmth of her fingers—opened in her hand to disclose a paper doll caught between the leaves. One of hers that she had painted with her father's help when she was eight. How long had he carried the doll about—and why? Maybe she had dropped it somewhere and he had picked it up, intending to return it to her. Maybe. She preferred to think though that the doll reminded him of his daughter and he had carried it about for reasons of sentiment.

What a strange child she had been. At an age when many girls were tomboys, she had played quietly in a corner with her paper dolls, making up stories about them. They were her "family," as the figures were in the Pryors' lithograph. But enough of ghosts, she told herself sternly. She had come to work.

The sun had a lazy warmth now, and there was almost no breeze. She wandered along the stream, noting trillium still in bloom and Dutchman's-breeches and there a jack-in-the-pulpit. She sat down on a boulder with the murmur of the creek peaceful and timeless in her ears. As she drew out her copy of Father's painting, she wondered fleetingly what had become of his many pictures. She had a vague recollection that Aunt Rhoda had persuaded Mr. Cleghorne to exhibit them for sale in the art store. If so, Mr. Teiler had probably bought *The Red Barn* there.

Swiftly she pushed him away from her thoughts as if he had been a troublesome mosquito and busied herself with the copy in her hand. Yes, right from this spot Father had painted, and she needed to change little really except the shadows and the color of the vine leaves on the stone fence and the bank of the creek to convey spring dampness and the lively bark of the trees. She began to sketch rapidly, a preliminary drawing that she could later follow for the final picture.

As she worked, she visualized her father with his students who sat on the dusty floor of the barn as he lectured on the repetition of color to unify a painting or any one of a dozen principles and threw in bits of his philosophy and told his jokes. And when his students had gone, he often walked along the creek for a while, head down as he reflected.

She could see him well enough, but oddly today she could not imagine his sauntering back again. A swarm of insects circled around her head, and she slapped at them from time to time in annoyance, and she blamed them that she could not concentrate sufficiently on Father.

A soft breeze sprang up, carrying with it a fragrance of wild locusts. From the village, church bells sounded in a jumbled peal. Ten-thirty o'clock or going on for eleven, she guessed, and began now to mix paints, making patches of color to be matched later. She longed to feel for just a short while that Father was there, looking over her shoulder, his chin pinched between thumb and forefinger as he appraised her work. He had such an expressive face that she'd never had to ask his opinion. She could always see for herself.

Pressing her paint cloth over her brush, she sat thoughtfully still. Of course, he would not come to her now—

even in imagination. Nor did she want his disgust, his scorn, his blistering words. Oh, he approved of her copying his work, yes. Rightly or wrongly, he believed she learned by studying his methods. But to enter such a painting in a contest and pass it off as her own? Jumping Judas, no!

"But it will be mine when I'm finished," she protested aloud and shifted her legs so violently she startled a frog. She watched it leap into the underbrush along the bank, and went on grumbling. Well, all right, so the original idea was not hers and the composition was not hers, the contest rules just called for paintings. And for mercy's sake, some artists copied photographs. She'd bet there'd be plenty such entries in the contest. What was the difference whether one painted from a snapshot or adapted a painting from another one? After all, she was making some changes. Well, all right. Not many. But some. And anyway, if her father were a responsible parent, she would not have to depend on a contest for an education. And anyway, *just this once.*

She swatted at the insects. "Go away! Go away!" she cried and set stubbornly to work again. The sun was noticeably warmer, and the shadows short and sharp when she finished at last. She checked and double-checked her notes, then carried her paint pans and brushes down to the creek, and having cleaned them in turpentine, washed her hands in the water, letting it ripple coolly over her fingers. A chipmunk scuttled up a tree. A dirty ginger cat climbed over a broken fence in a clearing beyond the farthest bank and disappeared onto the road. Somewhere a fish plopped, and in the pool under the trees, minnows darted in squiggles of silver.

She did not believe she would ever come back and yet she was reluctant to leave. She scrambled up the bank, sat on the rock, and ate half of her sandwich. She ate an apple, started to wrap up the core to dispose of later, and then, feeling rebellious, tossed it into the creek where it landed with a splash and was pushed by the current under a stone.

Once more she descended to the stream, and scooping up the cold water, held it against her eyes. In a rush, memories flooded back, and she recalled how the last day while the van was loading, she had dashed off, crossed on the stepping stones to the other side. Beyond the fence she had climbed her favorite tree, and sitting in the hollow she had cried, ignoring the calls of her parents. She never knew how long they had searched nor how they had come to find her. But she did remember that somewhere here on the bank, Mother had forced Zenty down on her knees and splashed her face with the cold water. She had hated her mother for the final indignity. But squatting now on her heels, Zenty thought not of herself at fourteen, but of a child nearly hysterical with distress, of a woman ambivalent in her own feelings—determined to be right but unsure, angry at her sense of guilt, her unhappiness. *Something* had to be done to stop the child's weeping.

"Poor Mother," Zenty said. Oh, she ought never, never to have stirred up ghosts.

She clambered back to the rock, packed her kit, stood a moment looking at the barn. She had rather intended to hunt out old neighbors, but now she knew she would not. With kit in hand, she ran past the house and along the dusty road and did not slow down until she had rounded the bend and reached the woods. Near the crossroads, she sighted the bus and raced as she waved to the driver. He waited and she climbed aboard, panting.

Fifteen minutes later, she alighted at the drugstore in Green Meadows and was debating whether she had time for a cup of coffee when an obviously repainted yellow car drove up and a voice called, "Well, hey, I was right. What do you know?"

Instinctively, she swung her artist's kit back of her to hide it from Gyps. But, indeed, she was relieved to see him and to leave Wood Hollow Road and its memories behind.

And yet the morning had had its uses: She had scarcely thought of the Teilers at all.

ELEVEN

Giuseppe reached across the seat and opened the door for her, and she thought at once of Wig and how he always walked around the car and settled her in. Then determinedly she shut him out of her mind and began to question Gyps eagerly as he studied her. Why was he not at the seashore?

Oh, the shack, he said, was a hide-out for those times when the world was too much with him, late and soon, to misquote Wordsworth. Practically the whole Di Costa tribe lived in Green Meadows, but what was *she* doing there?

"Wait," he said before she could reply, "something's prickling in my mighty brain."

With a sly glance, she asked, "The way hands and feet prickle when they're asleep?"

"*No!* And any more such cracks, Miss Sperrow—

Sperrow!" His dark eyes lighted with his sudden discovery. "Arnold Sperrow's daughter. You," he said, pointing a finger that almost touched her nose, "were a little scarecrow of a kid with enormous eyes that looked so wistful, I always wanted to pat you on the head." Then abruptly: "What do you hear from your father?"

"You know him?" she exclaimed, dodging his question.

"Enough to know he's a nice guy. He understood that I had to help in our store, but he let me sit in on his classes free whenever I could get away. A fellow appreciates that sort of thing, especially when his own family thinks this art stuff is for Sundays only."

She was beginning to place him now. "I remember a Di Costa grocery on Montgomery Street, yes?"

"That's us."

"Sure. My father always traded there. And he'd let me pay the bill on Saturdays and then a man . . ." He was stooped over, she recalled, and her father said that Mr. Di Costa had arthritis.

". . . gave you a bag of candy," Gyps said.

"Licorice strings and pebbly hard balls with chewy centers."

"Mmmmm. Hmmmm."

"I used to suck one all the way home, and to make the candy last, I'd take it out of my mouth every few seconds. Drove my father nearly crazy."

Oh, there were good things to remember. Why did she not remember them more often?

"Do you still run the store?" she asked.

"My brothers do. They think I should, too. Artist, phooey! You want to be an artist, you have to fight everybody, including yourself." He eased the car away from the curb. "How did I get on that subject?" he asked.

For a while they rode in silence—past a filling station, an empty vegetable stand that a man was painting in anticipation of the season, over a bridge traversed by fishermen in high boots, past a cemetery where a woman was weeding a grave. Two bluejays flew before the car.

"Two for luck," Gyps said, rousing. "Zenty, are you bringing me luck? You're a comfortable gal to have around. You don't yak-yak-yak all the time."

"I was thinking I ought to. You don't seem altogether happy today."

"Who, me? Oh, I'm just a moody rascal. Look, there's my school. Do you mind if we stop a moment? I have something to deposit."

He turned the car into the driveway that led through an avenue of leafing trees to an old clapboard house that had apparently been converted into a school. It had wide eaves and small windows with paper tulips pasted on the inside of the farthest group. Spring flourished in the kindergarten, she judged. There was a pathetic gaiety about the flowers that reminded her of the red doors she and her father had painted on the Wood Hollow Road place. This house, too, needed painting, and its lines were marred by an ugly fire escape at the side that proclaimed the house to be no longer a home. She thought briefly of Mr. Teiler then and at once began to scrabble about mentally for something to fasten her attention to. Anything. The grass greening—and there, a blade left swinging as an insect jumped from one to another.

Gyps said, "I'll be only a moment." He fumbled at the trunk of the car and came back along the walk, lugging two canvases. She leaned across the car and called to him, but he did not answer her. He disappeared inside the house, and when he returned and climbed in behind the wheel, she said, "Were those paintings of yours?"

"Yep."

"Why didn't you let me see them?"

"They ain't me best, sweetie pie. For you only the best, see?"

"Oh, nonsense," she said.

"Oh, they'll jazz up the front office for the big do, I guess. We're entertaining parents, trying to jack up the enrollment." He waved his hand in front of his face as if shooing a fly. "Ach, let's get out of here."

He backed the car swiftly, then wheeled it forward with a crunch of gravel that sounded explosive in the mild, sunlit air. "I get psychic waves or something from this place lately."

"Why?"

"I don't know. Do you believe in hunches, Zenty?"

"Sometimes, yes."

"I've got one now, and I don't like it."

"About the school?"

"I'm not sure. I seem to be worrying, and I don't know about what."

"I have a theory about hunches," Zenty said, "especially the worrying kind. I think you've noticed something that is troubling you—only you don't remember noticing whatever it is, but still it needles you."

"Could be," Gyps said. "Well, there's plenty to notice around here. I'll bet there hasn't been a repair to the main building in ten years except when I came over one week end and replaced a couple of boards on the stairs."

"It's a private school?"

"Oh, sure. But as I said before—or did I?—let's talk about you."

"Let's not."

"Got a date tonight?"

She shook her head.

"What do you say we drive out to the golf course and then feast ourselves on hot dogs, hmmmm?"

She hesitated as she realized that somewhere in the back

of her mind all morning had been the hope that Wig would call. She glanced at her watch. Two o'clock. Well, if he had intended to phone, he had certainly done so by now, and she had missed him. Gyps was smiling sardonically, and she said quickly, "I have an essay to write for class tomorrow, that's all."

"I'll get you home early," Gyps promised.

"What's at the golf course? A tournament?"

"No. Driving range. Thought we'd practice a few swings. Okay?"

"Yes." Only she did wish Wig were along, too. Just as a foil for Gyps . . . that was all. Well, no, that was not all. In a way, she guessed, she was a coward about love. And when she thought of Mr. Teiler, worried that the girl from Elm Street might capture his precious son, she could bite hickory nuts in two. Why, she had never in all her life even so much as written a boy a note, except in answer to one from him. She never called boys on the telephone.

She traced a plaid square of her kilts absently. Suppose at the party, Eddie had not behaved like a clown. And suppose she had asked not Wig but Mr. Teiler to show her *The Red Barn,* would he like her any better now?

Gyps snapped his fingers before her eyes, and she jerked back startled. He began to hum *Beautiful Dreamer,* and she smiled at his profile, strongly outlined and even-featured. He ought to be on the stage, she decided, or starred in a movie with a Florentine background. She could quite imagine him in the role of a medieval artist. He enjoyed much that she did—art, music, the outdoors. Why was she not as excited or even as content with him as she was with Wig? As if anyone knew the answer to *that.*

"What's your essay about?" Gyps asked.

"I haven't given it any thought," she confessed. "Wig encourages autobiographical sketches."

"Shouldn't wonder," Gyps said. "Teiler's the sort who'd want to know all about his students. Now me . . . I just want the brats to come in and keep quiet and go away again."

"*Gyps!* I don't believe you."

"Don't you now? Well, I have to pretend to be hard-boiled, don't I? Otherwise I'd spoil the little cuties all to smithereens. Is Wig a pretty good teacher?" He glanced at her quickly and back at the road again as if hoping she might betray her own feelings about Wig.

"Yes, he really is. He appears to enjoy the—uh—expounding and—"

"Authority?" Gyps asked.

"Maybe that most of all," she admitted but felt disloyal even to assent.

"I'm not criticizing him," Gyps said hastily, "which, of

course, means that I am," he added with a grin. "But, no, I sort of envy him, to tell the truth. Me . . . I don't want to be bossed but neither do I want to boss. Too lazy, I guess. Teiler just naturally takes over."

"He's quite formal in the classroom. There's no doubt about who's teacher."

"That's what I mean," Gyps said. "Wig's what I call a good organization man. When he's in charge, he's in charge, but he knows how to bow to authority, too. Papa Teiler, for instance." He threw her another swift appraising glance.

She began marking her kilts again.

"I don't know what the old boy expects of Wig—that he become college president two hours and six seconds after he gets his Ph.D. probably," Gyps said. "I suspect that's why Wig keeps putting off returning to Yale."

"Do you think maybe he won't go back this fall?" she asked.

"I'm not taking any bets," Gyps said. "Hey, how did we get to talking about Teiler?"

"My essay."

"Oh, yeah, yeah. Well, you don't have to worry. He'd give you an *A* no matter what you wrote."

"Oh, no, indeed. Not Instructor Teiler. You get *A*'s only when you earn them."

"You, too?"

"Me, too."

"Are you sure?" Gyps thrust his tongue in his cheek.

"Yes, *sir.*"

"Like one of my old profs, huh?" Gyps said. "Always tougher on his favorites just to assure himself he was being fair. Nertz to that if they're pretty girls, I say. Pamper 'em —dumb or bright. Give 'em all *A*'s."

"Spoken like a man," Zenty said. She ought to feel flattered and feminine, she supposed, but at heart she still respected Wig for his integrity. Strange that in class he accorded her the dignity of a student who had to prove herself like any other. Outside school, though, he regarded her as . . . what? She certainly wished she knew. Or did she? Cinderella, according to Aunt Doris. Not that she said so outright—merely hinted. But trust Cuss Sperrow to pick up the hints. Zenty folded her hands in her lap. She wished the Cinderella notion had not occurred to her. Oh, wish, wish, wish! Did she ever do anything else? Sometimes she got awfully sick of herself.

The car approached the northern end of Mt. St. Clare and paced a fairway of gentle mounds, long undulating greens, a pond, a wooded fringe, and then, as Gyps flipped on the directional signal, turned right at the sign with the burning bush that announced the exclusive Flaming Bush Club.

Zenty sat up abruptly. "Oh, not here!" she exclaimed.

"Why not?" Gyps asked.

"But—but—are you a member?"

"Who, me?"

"Well, are you?"

"You thought I was poor folks, huh? You're so right. But, see, I used to caddy here and sometimes I still work in the shop. The pro and the manager know me and they figure . . . this guy, Di Costa . . . he's an artist. Who can tell? Some day we may wish we'd been nice to him. So they are."

Yes, but what did others think? After all, the club house and the golf links and the driving range behind the shop belonged to the members—not to the manager nor the pro. She hated to trespass anywhere. She sat worriedly biting her thumbnail as Gyps parked the car. He opened the door for her.

"Now if you want to make like a member," he said, "you'll march straight into the manager's office and complain that last Monday the flowers on your table were cerise and you specifically asked for magenta."

"And what will the manager say to *me?*"

"Believe me, gorgeous, he has all the answers on IBM file cards."

"Oh, Gyps!" she said, laughing despite her uneasiness.

"Come on," he said. "You a golfer?"

"No."

"So now I teach you in six million easy lessons." He disappeared around the back of the shop and as she waited she looked off along the one stretch of fairway visible from the steps toward the tiny figures moving relentlessly ahead. From this distance, no one was anyone—only patches of color: a bright blue hat, a pair of dark green shorts, and a beige blouse, and there a yellow scarf heading into the woods in search of a lost golf ball. Now two pairs of slacks and two sports shirts joined in the quest, and none of them knew nor cared that Zenty Sperrow, uninvited, watched from their private domain.

But *she* cared, and she was not comfortable even when Gyps, on returning with drivers and bags full of golf balls, assured her that no lessons were scheduled for the afternoon and so the range belonged to Zenty and Gyps. He showed her the hold on the club, the wrist motion, the back swing. Sometimes she imagined Wig there beside her, Wig's hand on hers, Wig's voice. Gyps demonstrated the swing with a relaxed ease. The club cracked. The ball sang as it flew straight and low to the mesh fence at the back of the lot. Now and then, a light breeze stirred her hair against her flushed face. From somewhere beyond, where a brook ran, came the musty smell of rotting vegetation. And there was a peacefulness in all, but she could not relax.

"Are you always so earnest about everything?" Gyps asked, and he seemed to her then so like a child who accepted the world as his that she could not tell him her training rebelled against intrusion where she did not belong.

The shadows of the fence speckled the field as the sun swung toward the west. Gyps went out to pick up golf balls, and she was practicing her swing, trying to hit a tee, when she became aware that someone sat on the steps of the shop and watched her. She stopped and waited for Gyps, and a blister on her palm began to sting. He sauntered back, stooping now and then to retrieve a ball she had hit. The figure on the porch stirred, and Derek called, "Gyps."

The two moved together behind Zenty. She turned as Gyps, laying a hand on Derek's shoulder, peered closely at the mustache. "I do believe it's grown," he said. "What are you using?"

"Eyebrow pencil," Derek said cheerfully. "Great stuff if you ever need it."

"Shan't," Gyps said. "I could grow a beard that would put a bear to shame."

"Quit bragging and stow that stuff away. We're all going over to the hamburger jernt."

"Who's we-all?"

"Mur and Joss and Archer and me."

"Archer?" Gyps exclaimed with a jerk of his head. "Where's the little shepherdess?"

Derek puckered his mouth and studied the toe of his shoe. "If you mean my sister, how should I know?"

Zenty glanced swiftly from one face to the other—Derek's embarrassed and Gyps's puzzled.

Gyps grunted, and Derek said, "Uh, look—uh, don't— If I were you, I wouldn't make any cracks to Archer."

"So hokey. Who's making cracks? Dumb I am like a beast."

"Yeah, I know. Are you coming with us?"

"Sure, soon as I get the grime off my hands. That is— Okay, Zenty?"

She nodded, and Derek said, "Oh, *hi!*" as if he had just that instant spotted her, but there was a falseness to his tone of surprise. Gyps noticed and without moving his head looked first at her and then at Derek, and as Gyps took the driver from her, he muttered something about the competition that she did not altogether hear and did not want to. She was worried now about Archer and Nonie— afraid that they had quarreled.

With Gyps and Derek, she walked along past the greens toward the club house and was mildly surprised to discover that it looked on the outside like a child's notion of a Tudor castle and inside had the air of a country hotel.

She had expected to find Mur and Joss in the powder room, but found instead only a lone attendant, seated near the mirrors that reflected a Victorian wallpaper, profuse with tumbled roses and violets. The uneasiness of an intruder disturbed Zenty again, and she fumbled the soap and dropped her comb and was sure the woman watched her curiously.

Out again in the hallway of carved oak beams and plastered ceilings, she waited beside an open doorway for the two young men and thought of Archer and Nonie. Zenty had no notion whether they were either pinned or engaged. She had not noticed a ring, but then girls like Nonie who everyone knew could afford a dozen diamonds sometimes preferred only a wedding band. For that matter, so did Zenty. As an engagement token, she would choose —if she had a choice—a slim chain ring that would serve as a guard for the wedding band later. If I ever marry, she reminded herself crossly.

A drift of scent roused her, and she became aware that couples in evening garb were filtering into the club house. And where *were* the boys and Mur and Joss? She glanced into the adjoining room and was suddenly arrested by a painting over the mantel. Gulls—not with every feather depicted. Gulls *suggested* in flight—a picture of windswept sea and sky, of space and motion and freedom.

She heard Gyps behind her talking to Derek and turned

to inquire for the artist just as Archer, walking toward them, stopped abruptly. His long face grew painfully scarlet, and the outline of his fists bulged his pockets. And even before she turned back, she knew that Nonie had entered the hall. She wore a white dinner dress and carried a stole over her arm, and she might herself have been a painting by Sargent. Wig, following, almost stepped on her heels. He, too, stopped shortly and touched Nonie gently on the elbows, and the touch that was not for Zenty ran through her like a pain.

Then Wig saw her. She had time to note his astonishment, his swift appraisal of the group, before she lifted her hand in a discreet wave and somehow managed a smile.

TWELVE

She had long ago learned that hurts had to be fought before they subsided. One tried to ignore the ache and pretended gaiety and said, "I don't care. I really don't care." One indulged in futile dreams of comfort and revenge. And the whole process had to be gone through with or the bleakness never would end. She wished she did not have to think. She wished she could go straight home and sleep and wake up as serenely as if nothing had disturbed her. But, of course, she could not.

And so she joked with the gang on the way to Gyps's car. Out at the hamburger place on the shore road—amidst charcoal and onion and pickle smells—she laughed merrily at Archer and he at her as if they were vying for a prize to the gayest of them all. She chattered away to Gyps as he drove her home. After he had left her, she

stood a moment in the hall. Casually she glanced at the
table for telephone messages, and finding only a note from
her aunts that they had gone to a movie, she told herself
she had never really supposed Wig might have called before he invited Nonie to dinner. Why should he not escort
Nonie anywhere he chose? After all, he had made Zenty
Sperrow no promises of love.

She hurried upstairs, and when she had bathed and put
on her crinkly flowered pajamas, she hunted a murder
mystery and tried to read—the same page over and over.
Tomorrow she would see Wig. How should she behave
so that he would not guess her feelings? Perhaps she ought
to saunter into class with another student—appear so engrossed in feminine conversation as to be unaware of Wig.
Or joke with the boy across the aisle until class began. Or
arrive early, maybe, settle down, and read without glancing
up when Wig came in. Or ought she, possibly, to slip in at
the last moment and be so preoccupied that she would
answer absently, coolly when he called the roll? "Miss
Sperrow." "Here." She might even sound a bit bored.

She wanted to *hurt* him with her indifference.

After a time, she fell asleep only to awaken long past
midnight in panic. She had not written her essay, and
what was more, she had given it no thought since mentioning it to Gyps. She sat up in bed and tried to describe
her bus trip that morning. The essay had no point but, she

told herself defiantly, she did not care. She did not care
about anything at all. She fell asleep with the light on,
awoke at four and turned it off, and in the morning
scribbled out a last paragraph.

She arrived at school with flutterings in her stomach.
And then to her amazement, Wig never looked at her
once. His glance moved leisurely all around her, over her
head, to the back of the room, to the front, to the left, to
the right. But her seat might as well have been empty
for all he appeared to see her. At the end of the period,
when she dropped her paper on his desk, one of the boys
was talking to him. She had the impression for a moment
that Wig was about to turn to her, but by then the tears
were so close to her eyes that she hurried away. She
walked rapidly, angrily about the Square before going on
to the clinic. There, she had barely hung up her coat and
stowed away her bag when for the first time the thought
occurred to her that Wig had meant to hurt her as she
had hoped to hurt him. Could he be a little jealous of
Gyps? *Wig?* The possibility mollified her for a time. By
evening, the message pads were covered on the back with
her name and his—with like letters crossed out in the old
game of friendship, love, marriage, hate:

Cassandra Sparrow
Ludwig Tiley

But since the unscratched letters counted out to *hate,* her fortune-telling scarcely cheered her.

All Tuesday he haunted her. She awoke several times in the night as excited over class the next day as a child who at once anticipates and dreads a party—and then to her dismay she overslept.

When she arrived at school, out of breath and with cheeks flushed, the clock on the church tower was just beginning to strike the hour nine minutes late as always. Class, of course, had started. She tiptoed to her seat, her left shoe squeaking with every step, and sat down gingerly. As she settled her purse on the floor, slipped out of her coat, and opened her notebook, silence crowded in all around her. Sounds of a hedge clipper drifted in with the smell of burning brush. She was warm and uncomfortable from hurrying and . . . from embarrassment, darn it. She gazed steadily at her pen. Someone tittered, and Wig slid a ruler across his desk.

She looked at him then, hesitantly, ready to turn away, but he was staring rigidly at the offender. She thought, the great stone face, and almost snickered in her nervousness.

"Let's stop the childishness right now," Wig said, "and I'll start over for the benefit of late-comers." (Me, Zenty thought indignantly.) "You'll all do well to listen, and I mean all." (Including Zenty Sperrow, *A* student. Fair-haired girl. Or was.)

Zenty settled back and waited, and secretly she knew she was enjoying in an unhappy way her annoyance at him. He squared the record book with the edge of the blotter, his eyes squinted.

"As I started to say ten minutes ago, I'm through tolerating sloppiness in this class. You are sloppy in your attendance, in your lack of punctuality, in the condition of your papers. If they're not smudged with ink, they're typed so faintly I could sooner read them in Sanskrit."

He looked deliberately around the room. His glance met hers and moved away. "Don't you ever replace typewriter ribbons?" he demanded.

Zenty started to shift. Her forearm stuck to her notebook and came away with a sucking sound. Jostled by the movement, her pen rolled. Hastily she caught it. By then, her pulse was hammering in her throat, and she had an urge to giggle. She drew in a deep breath as Wig's voice struck out crisply again.

"You're sloppy in your punctuation. Judging from your papers, the use of the apostrophe is a lost art. Worst of all, you are sloppy in your syntax. And frankly, I'm fed up."

He shoved back the attendance book with his fist. "From now on late-comers will be marked absent, messy papers will be graded zero, and those of you who need them will have extra assignments in punctuation and grammar. Any student who does not know enough to put a period at the end of a sentence does not belong in college."

Again his intensely blue eyes considered the entire class. "I don't ask for lofty writing," he said, "merely honest, accurate communication that respects the language."

Outdoors an airplane droned briefly overhead and was gone, and the clip-clop of the hedge shears began again. Within the classroom no one stirred. Momentarily, at least, the freshman rhetoric students of Mt. St. Clare College were, if not intimidated, at least subdued. And despite Zenty's jumbled emotions—which she herself could not always sort out—she was now mainly amused at a young Mr. Teiler she had never seen before. This was not Wig. This was Instructor Ludwig Hellman Teiler III. She could barely restrain a smile, but then he said, "You haven't many weeks left to pull up your grades," and at thought of the school year's ending, she sobered at once.

He picked up a piece of chalk and stared at it. She could let herself imagine that he, too, was regretting the term's end. But was he? No other class would ever be for her as exciting as this, but for him there would be many, probably more stimulating, with students more talented to begin with. He tossed the chalk onto the blackboard ledge and said, "I trust I have made myself clear." Then reaching across the desk with a pile of papers, he handed them to a boy in a front seat, told him to select his own, and to pass on the rest.

Now suddenly she was apprehensive. That last essay of hers on the bus ride had been scrawled. It had been—oh gosh, she did not know what. She waited now for the progression of the papers around the room as if they were the lighted fuse of a giant firecracker. Silly, too. Meanwhile, Wig began roll call. Albright. Anderson. Miss Baumgartner. Miss Caparelli. By the time he had reached the *S*'s, Zenty sat frowning in disbelief at a large red *D* at the top of her paper. Never in any English class—despite poor grades in some other subjects—had she received less than a *B*. Even *B*'s she resented. She touched her cheeks with her palms, then lowered them immediately, aware that she was betraying herself. In her chagrin, she did not hear her name called, and when she looked up, Wig was closing the record book. A smile, briefer than the wink of an eye, twitched at his lips and was gone. She could forgive him anything, she thought, but the smile.

For the rest of the period, she scribbled notes angrily as Wig lectured. She did not laugh at his dry wit, and somehow she controlled the constant impulse to glance up at him. The moment the bell rang, she grabbed her books and purse and hurried through the door. Out in the hall, a boy with sandy hair and freckles caught up with her.

"Hey," he said, "I sort of think old Ludwig wanted to talk to you. He was watchin' you leave."

"Well, I'm not clairvoyant," Zenty said, "and there's nothing wrong with his voice."

"You can say that again," the boy told her. "He sure blew his stack, didn't he?" He reached for her books. "Where's your next class?"

"Over at the clinic," she told him. "Thanks all the same."

At the corner across from the church, she stopped and pulled out the offending essay. Wig had not marked a single error in spelling or punctuation or grammar, but at the bottom of the second page he had written: "Diffuse. Disconnected. Pointless. What were you trying to say, Zenty?"

Brooding, she stepped out into the street, but dodged back quickly to let a car pass. She suddenly had no notion of what to do until the clinic doors opened. She would not in any case sit and brood in the churchyard. Abruptly she headed for the Square and there sauntered from window to window, seeing but not really noticing what lay behind them. She forgot time, and, rousing, had to run most of the way to the old municipal building. Once inside the switchboard room, she tore the paper into confetti and tumbled the bits into the wastebasket, then shoved the basket around where she could not see it.

She would not think of Wig for the rest of the day. She would think of . . . going to New York! Hey, there was an idea! If she could not find the money for art school in the fall, maybe she could somehow manage enough to tide her over in New York until she got a job—one that would use her talents. There had to be one somewhere, and she could take courses at night. In her excitement, she flipped the wrong button, disconnecting an outside call. She decided then to tend to her work.

All day the switchboard lights flashed and buzzed. By night she felt as if she had been cooped up in a hive but at least she had been busy—so busy, in fact, that she forgot her new plan. And anyway, what use was there merely to substitute one dream for another? She stood as always in the freshness of the evening air, and listened to the church chimes. Tonight the ivy shone with a glossy brilliance and threw sharp shadows where the late sunlight burnished the red brick. A vignette to paint if only she could express what she felt that instant with the church bell striking the hour.

Oh, her father was right. Spring was a beguiler, full of promises never kept. Yet if Wig were to happen along now, she might—she just might—forgive both him and spring. She glanced up and down the street and did not see him. She sauntered home, watchful for his car, and did not see it. Not then nor the next night.

On Friday, she arrived at school early just as Wig, later than usual—tanned and blond and immaculate in a navy blue suit—swung around the corner of the library toward the main building. She walked faster and he noticeably slowed down, and when she had caught up with him, he said, "Good morning."

She said, "Good morning."

They went on, side by side, in silence, and she was doggoned if she would be the first to break it. By an odd coincidence then, she glanced up at him out of the corners of her eyes just as he glanced down at her. He burst into laughter, and presently she began to giggle.

As they neared the entrance, he said, "You deserved that grade, you know."

"All right. You don't have to remind me."

"I never thought *you'd* be a sulker," he said.

"I'm not!" she exclaimed indignantly. "But I am annoyed because I'm never late and you needn't—"

"You were last Wednesday."

"Only that once, and you needn't have embarrassed me while I—"

"Fiddled with your purse and your coat and your books and your notebook and your pen and held up everybody."

"Oh, I didn't really. You were just in a foul mood."

He smiled his slow grin. "Ye-es, I was, wasn't I?" he said cheerfully, as if the notion had not even occurred to him before and he now found it amusing. "But I'll tell you something, Zenty. I went over your paper three times to be sure I was being fair."

"Oh, yes, I know that old bit," she said. "The *D* hurt you more than it did me."

"Who said so? I don't remember feeling a twinge. All the same, I don't want my star pupil slipping so near finals. So snap out of whatever's ailing you, will you?"

"*Oh*-kay," she said.

"I still don't understand what happened to you, Zenty. Why would you turn in a paper that said nothing—absolutely nothing?"

She chewed the inside of her lip as she debated what to say. After all, she thought, maybe he ought to know without telling. "I was upset last weekend," she said.

"That makes two of us then," Wig muttered. She studied her thumbnail, noting absently three tiny white spots like the points of a triangle. Why did one always have to fence? Why could she not ask outright without embarrassment whether he'd been disturbed because of her—whether he had missed her over vacation, maybe, more than he had expected to—or whether he had perhaps been a little jealous of Gyps? One had to be adroit, and she supposed rightly so. Still, she sometimes thought that a few honest questions and honest answers might in the end spare everyone trouble. At least, one would know where one stood.

Wig said, "I made a quick trip to Yale on Wednesday, left immediately after class and stayed over until last night

. . . or rather this morning." He stifled a yawn and grinned at her.

"You don't look beat," Zenty observed and after a pause asked, "Were you glad to get back to your own campus for a while?"

He hesitated and then said, "The students seem more mature there."

She and Wig were walking along the corridor now, and as they passed a bust of Shakespeare set in a niche, she noticed that somebody had tossed a beanie onto old William's head, where the cap rested jauntily over one eyebrow.

"Not much of this sort of thing," Wig said. "Oh, the kids play pranks, but more subtle ones, cleverer. I guess," he added. But he had not, she noticed, answered her question.

"Are we all through scrapping?" he asked. "Or shall we continue over dinner tonight?"

"Bad for the digestion," she said and added quickly, "Let's get indigestion."

"Very good," he said. "Where shall I pick you up?"

"At the aunts'."

He nodded, smiled at her, and held the door for her as they passed on into the classroom. So there she was again, accepting his hasty invitations. What was she—his star pupil or the little Sperrow kid or his best girl? She wished she knew.

THIRTEEN

The evening started out pleasantly and was at first full of little happy incidents. She and Wig ate at an inn near Green Meadows where she had met Gyps the previous Sunday. And as they were leaving, she pointed out a container with wooden teeth that held menus.

"A cranberry rake," Wig explained, "and as far as I'm concerned should be used for raking cranberries. Don't tell me you're the sort of gal who sticks flowers in coffee-pots and grows plants in birdcages."

"Mmmmm, no, I guess not," she said, not having considered before whether she was or not.

"Well, thank heaven for that," he said, as if her taste in interior decoration might matter to him in the future. She savored the idea for quite a while.

And then there was an instant as he pushed open the

door for her, standing close behind her with his hand on her shoulder, that she sensed Wig's protectiveness. As she gazed up at him to prolong the moment, he studied her face, and she saw a tenderness in his eyes, fleeting but there.

He said, "You're adorable," but so softly she thought at first he had said she was terrible, and then because they were blocking the entranceway, he propelled her gently into the spring night. And what he had said she stored up to think about and think about.

A full moon that had been a wraith at dusk shone behind the feathery trees and touched the new leaves with silver. In the garden back of the parking lot, dampness routed the fragrances of the earth and mingled them with a spicy smell that Zenty could not identify and it therefore seemed intended specially for her and Wig.

As he helped her into the car, he said, "Shall we dance, madam? Or bowl? Or roller skate? Or shoot ducks?"

"All four, of course," she said, thinking he was fooling. But he was not, and after a fifteen-minute ride toward Buttercup Lake, they stopped at the Grand Casino—a massive new glassed-in building that offered various amusements. She danced with Wig to the beat of a tinny piano played by a tiny woman with crisp red curls and obviously powerful fingers, for the music made up in volume what it lacked in tone. Zenty danced with her eyes shut and her hair touching Wig's cheek, and she was blissful. But then the floor became crowded, and Wig steered her upstairs to the bowling alley that smelled of dust and chalk and stale cigarette smoke. And there she rolled duck pins in her stockinged feet. When the game ended, and he had won—as, of course, she had expected him to—Wig said, with a glance at her heeled shoes, "No skating tonight, but come on, we'll shoot ducks."

And they did, in a gallery around the back where a heavy-faced man sat on a stool behind a counter and chewed gum. He looked bored until Wig shot down a row of ducks in motion. The man pivoted around then and inquired, "Marines?"

"Navy," Wig said.

"What did you shoot? Whale?"

"Trained on a duck pond," Wig said.

"Wouldn't surprise me none," the man told him and later parted with a raggedy-ann doll that he said was a sample and he didn't know as he could get no more. But anything for a lady that was stuck with the Navy.

She and Wig started back then toward the Green Meadows road to Mt. St. Clare. They talked of many things, and eventually she spoke again of his trip to Yale and asked him to describe his campus. She loved campuses. And he said that she romanticized them, that they were not necessarily so Elysian as she imagined. But she still thought they were like immense estates, housing immense families whose members were all intellectually attuned and stimulating to each other. Ordinary horse sense told her she was wrong, of course, because human beings were human beings everywhere, but she did not always listen to sense.

Hesitantly, she asked, "You are going back in the fall?"

He shrugged.

"Professor, you have not answered my question."

He laughed. "Maybe I didn't intend to answer your question." He explained then that the chairman of his committee—his advisor—was taking a leave of absence beginning in February and Wig could not decide whether to wait another year before returning or whether to knock himself out trying to finish up during the fall term— whether he could actually. That was the problem. He did not mind the work.

She believed him—the part about the work anyway. But she also recalled what Gyps had surmised—that Wig was hedging against his father's expectations as surely as if the elder Mr. Teiler had ordered his son to become dean or college president the moment he earned his doctorate. And always under her other thoughts was the wish that Wig might be delaying because of her.

For some time as they talked, she was aware of a red glow along the horizon, but only in the same sense that she was aware of the night and the deep shadows and pools of moonlight. Suddenly beyond an open field a billow of black smoke mushroomed through the glare.

"Hey!" Wig exclaimed. "Where is *that?*"

"I've no idea," Zenty said, but the pit of her stomach tightened as if it knew what she did not. She tried to orient herself, but she had never possessed a maplike mind or much sense of direction. Off there beyond the horizon might lie the red barn and the house on Wood Hollow Road. She wondered whether she would really care if they burned. Or whether she would experience a tremendous sense of relief as if the memories that pulled her emotions in a constant tug-of-war might disappear with the destruction of the old place.

Far off, sirens wailed. The car traveled over a bridge where the stream reflected ripples of moonlight, past a cemetery where gleaming white tombstones cast shadowy patches. The smoke hung like a menacing cloud with the red glare showing through eerily. A flame suddenly pierced the blackness.

"You don't suppose . . ." Wig said without mentioning what it was that she did not suppose and then said, "Let's hope not."

"Let's hope not what?" she asked, but at that moment Wig spotted a policeman ahead. With a flashlight the officer motioned the car onto a side road. Wig drove for about the length of a city block past a farmyard, then pulled off onto the grass.

"I'm worried," Wig said. "That could be Gyps's school."

"Oh, no!" Zenty cried.

"Let's walk back and see."

Still clutching her doll, she climbed out of the car without waiting for Wig.

"We'll have to duck through the woods," Wig said, "or we'll be in everyone's hair—police, firemen, the whole lot."

"Oh, no, we won't," Zenty protested.

"That's what everyone thinks," Wig told her. "I was on a volunteer fire department one summer, and, boy, we needed a sprinkling truck with long sprays to run interference."

She listened, but he had taken her hand to lead her through the cars that were now inching along the side street and she enjoyed again a sense of dependence on him. He held tightly to her as they crossed the main road and found a path along a stream. The sky was so bright now that every pebble and broken twig strewn over the ground cast a shadow. Occasionally puffs of white smoke shot off into the air.

"Can't be the school after all," Wig said, but as they stepped out into the clearing, he added quickly, "But it is!"

"Oh, dear!" Zenty said in distress.

Flames shot out of windows lately decorated with paper

tulips and licked upward toward the roof. Gray ash coated the fire escape and from time to time fluttered like dirty snowflakes.

"Oh, dear," she said again. "Oh, Wig, I wonder if Gyps knows."

At some distance from the school, among a group of outbuildings, men were leading away horses that shied and bucked in rebellion. Their frightened neighs penetrated the continuous crackle. One horse broke loose and galloped toward the still untouched barn. Men shouted as they converged on the scared beast. After maneuvering him from side to side, they managed to head him back toward the road.

Wig said, "Zenty, I'm going to leave you for a while, and I want you to stay right here."

For a moment, she was a child again, wearing socks and her very best dress and her hair in a ponytail, and Wig was instructing her to sit on the bench and watch the swans while he chased after the balloon vendor. And there was a fleeting memory of happiness, but of something else, too—a belief that some day she would grow up, and then Wig would treat her as a lady. She suppressed a brief and ridiculous rise of resentment.

"Zenty," he said.

"Yes, I heard you," she told him. "Are you—are you going to help with the horses?"

"With whatever I can. They may shoo me back. But you stay right here and don't try to come any nearer."

"All right," she said, and watched him run across the field—again puzzled by her ambivalent feelings toward Wig.

Smoke drifted low like fog, and the air had now become so acrid with the smell that at times she buried her nose in the doll's yarn hair. In a sudden roar, a side of the roof on the main building collapsed. She clutched the doll tighter, fascinated by the spectacle of fire. Now another section of the school gave way, easing down with the lazy speed of piled snow sliding. Sparks shot up like fireflies, and a blazing timber arched away and fell. Around her voices murmured. Others besides her and Wig had dodged through the woods. She peered around to see if she could spot Gyps, and her mind, independent of her preoccupation with her search, murmured over and over, poor Gyps, poor Gyps. But sympathy—pity—did not touch her—only a kind of nervous excitement.

Now the flames died down, and the hiss of the water as it struck the hot embers could be heard clearly. Occasionally still a small pop like the muffled shot of a gun exploded in the air, and a puff of white smoke arose. She was only partly aware of dark figures hurrying across the school grounds toward the clearing until Wig said, "Zenty," so close to her that she started. He smelled heavily of smoke. "Gyps hasn't come by, has he? I thought I saw him heading this way."

"No," she said. "Were you able to help?"

"Some, I guess," he said. "We carried stuff out of the barn and I held the hose with a couple of other guys while we played it on the side of the barn where the sparks were drifting. Everything's about under control now, but I wish I could find Gyps."

"You might if you turned around," a voice said behind them, and there stood Gyps, his shoulders drooping wearily in the half light of the moon. "Better not come too close though," he cautioned. "I'm covered with grime."

"Are you all right?" Wig asked. "What a lousy business . . . this."

And Zenty said, "I'm awfully sorry, Gyps."

"Yeah," Gyps agreed in a tired voice.

"Where were you?" Wig asked. "I looked for you."

"Oh, all over—carting stuff out of the south side of the building before the fire got around there, and then we trekked the horses down to some guy's pasture. What a mess."

"You're sure you're all right?" Wig asked.

"Yeah. Yeah."

"Well, look, you and Zenty wait by the road while I fetch the car, and I'll drive you home."

"Thanks, but my heap's around here somewhere."

"Well, let's at least get you a cup of coffee."

"Heh! You haven't seen me in the light. Even the joints around here wouldn't let me in." He rubbed his forehead with the back of his wrist. "Thanks all the same. I'll just hie me home and take a bath." The mere thought appeared to revive him.

He said to Zenty, "What are you doing with the doll, kid?"

"Little girls always carry dolls," Wig said, and then turning the subject away from her, "What were those puffs of smoke? Did you have a chem lab?"

"Yes, but I've a notion they came from cases of soft drinks we stored in the basement for the big wingding we intended to throw. Say, Zenty, didn't I tell you I had a hunch?"

"Yes, you did," she agreed.

"Of course, I did not anticipate fire," Gyps said. "It was the enrollment that had me worried, I believe. Wa-ay daown. You can bet we're out of business now, but at least no one's hurt."

"Well, yes, I suppose, you may as well be philosophical," Wig said. "You have a contract, Gyps?"

"Oh, sure—until June. But then, fini. So now I job-hunt."

They started back over the uneven ground and onto the path now heavily shadowed by the trees.

"This is no time to mention it, I suppose," Wig said, "but about your boat painting . . . Hadn't you better enter it in my father's contest?"

"The boat painting," Gyps said gloomily, "is gone with the blaze."

"*What!*"

"Yeah, *what!* I should have listened to you."

"Yes, you should have. Were you using it for class demonstration?"

"Naw. Loaned it for the big rinky-tink."

"Well, doggone you, put in a claim for it, boy. The place must be insured."

"I guess so."

Zenty had bent her head over her doll, and now she stumbled, and for a frightening moment she struggled not to fall. Gyps and Wig both grabbed for her, steadied her.

"Okay?" Wig asked.

"Mmmmm. Hmmmm." Outside she was fine. But inside she was—oh, not just shaken by that instant of fear— but something more. Briefly, as she'd heard that Gyps's painting was gone, she had felt, not just relief, but an actual satisfaction. And now she was ashamed of herself. The reaction was human enough, she supposed, but even so, there were times when she did not much admire the human condition.

Gyps blew her a kiss as he left, and she looked worriedly after him until Wig urged her through the dispersing crowd toward the car. He, too, appeared preoccupied, and she sat beside him, silent and still troubled as they rode away.

FOURTEEN

Zenty did not fall asleep at once that night.

To begin with, Doris's employer, Mr. Keel of the Blue Gull Gift Shop, had developed hepatitis and been rushed to the hospital. Aunt Doris had gone immediately to stay with his wife. And Aunt Rhoda, who had long hankered for a room of her own, perversely decided that her niece should occupy the empty twin bed.

"I've been brain-washed," Aunt Rhoda said.

And that, Zenty thought afterward as she lay wakeful and listened to her aunt's sonorous breathing, was precisely why she had to get away to school in the fall. One did become brain-washed or conditioned like Pavlov's dogs or simply molded to the rut. The longer one waited, the less chance one had to break away. Who could blame her for taking advantage of the contest? Undoubtedly Gyps would enter a painting now. With no contract to tie him down, he could propitiously use the money for more schooling before hunting a new job . . . *if* he won.

Well, and if *she* won, it was not for her to be concerned about Gyps, she told herself. After all, what was a contest but rivalry? If he was the better artist, then let him convince the judges. And if he would not paint to please, that was his business. Zenty Sperrow did not need to abide by Gyps's rules nor her father's either, for that matter.

She kicked off part of her covers.

She told herself once more that the barn painting, when finished, would be her work, and so, all right, Father would say the lady protested too much. She *did not care.* The painting—adapted from her preliminary sketch— was well along. It sat in an old north-lighted storeroom that the Pryors often let her use. She could not abandon the picture now—and to that her father would certainly agree. He despised unfinished paintings, standing about like the visible ghosts of one's own timidity or laziness. And besides, there was no time to plan another one all her own.

She pulled the covers back up again and was still arguing with herself, protesting, too, that she was *not* rationalizing, when she finally fell asleep.

On Saturday, she finished *Barn in Springtime* except

for the few touches that she always added after she had left a painting for a while and come back to it afresh. Would she ever, ever paint as well as her father did? Would she ever capture his delicacy? Still, her technique resembled his and her work had a freedom, almost a gaiety. She thought she *had* caught the spirit of spring, maybe even some of its promise in the contrast between the old barn and the reawakened earth. Well, she could only hope so.

On Sunday as she started off to visit her mother, Zenty had lost much of her uneasiness and she was rather pleased with herself. But as always, the moment she rang the bell, a heaviness weighed on her.

Mom was in Hory's room, and the maid told Zenty to go on up. She found the boy sitting in a chair by the window, pouring sunflower seeds into a bird-feeding trough which Mom held for him. Everything about the boy was sharp and thin—his profile, his long head, angular shoulders, and skinny arms. Once he turned and rapped loudly on his chair and a quick swish of furry tail flapped through the partly opened window and disappeared. He complained fretfully that the squirrels chased away the birds.

Then suddenly he noticed the girl and let out a shout. Mom started and said, "My land, Zenty, you might have knocked."

"I did," Zenty said.

And Hory went on calling for her to come look at his bird station and his new records. He had a great new book, too, and she could start reading to him from the beginning.

Mom's expression changed suddenly to anger, and she said sharply, "No, she cannot." She glared, not at the boy, but at Zenty. "Your aunt's coming up in a minute, and she can read to you—though why you can't be quiet and listen to your records and watch the birds . . ."

"Well, I can't," Hory said, his voice rising. "My aunt fumbles and mumbles, and I want Zenty to read."

"And you'll get all worked up and won't sleep again tonight and neither will I." Mother's sturdy complexion that seldom showed tiredness *was* smudged under the eyes. "Zenty came to see me, and if you don't behave, she will leave right now."

"No," Hory screamed, and grabbing a pillow from behind him, he flung it at Mrs. Sperrow. She stood rigidly straight and let the pillow glance off her shoulder. He reached back of him for another. Zenty rushed forward to stop him, but he shoved her with an unexpected strength that pushed her against the wall. The pillow sailed through the air and hit Mrs. Sperrow in the stomach, and still she did not move. Now he reached for a book, and with a cry, Zenty rushed forward again and clutched his arm. The book fell and he struggled to shake her off. The brief skirmish exhausted him. He drooped suddenly and began to cry. Instantly Mrs. Sperrow sprang past the bed and motioned Zenty out of the way, then stood looking down at the boy. He put both arms around Mrs. Sperrow's waist and rested his head against her.

She soothed him in a gentle scolding voice, and Zenty noticed how precisely right it was for the sickroom, not commiserating, not falsely cheerful, just everyday, matter-of-fact as if all were right with the world. When he had quieted, Mrs. Sperrow picked up the pillows and settled them again behind his back. She fetched a wet cloth and towel from the bathroom and patted his face. He submitted like a very small child.

Zenty, who had never witnessed his tantrums before, watched her mother in amazement and wondered how she had the patience. How did she endure his bad humor? Not only his but that of all the frightened, cantankerous sick to whom Mother had ministered these many years? Zenty herself felt sure she could not. Nor could Father. Yet had they not the conceit to consider themselves rather superior to Mother because of their love of books and the arts, because of their articulateness? It occurred to Zenty then that there were many kinds of intelligence and she ought to respect them all for what they were.

Only . . . Doggone it! Mom *was* unreasonable. She had

a positive *thing* about Zenty's reading to Hory—or reading to Zenty, for that matter. Morosely she retreated to the downstairs and awaited her mother.

After a time, Mrs. Sperrow came in. She had changed her dress and wore a copper-colored crepe that brought out the highlights in her hair. A copper medallion hung from a chain around her neck, and small replicas clung to her ear lobes.

She said, "Where's Wig? You were out with him last Sunday, weren't you? At least, you weren't home."

"Who told you I wasn't?"

"Nobody. A man called here for you, said he'd already phoned the Pryors' and you weren't there. Don't ask me who because I don't know. The old lady took the message, and she gets everything confuddled."

Wig, Zenty thought. Oh, gosh, maybe! He had tried to reach her and, failing, invited Nonie to the club—as a sort of family obligation to help cheer her after a lovers' quarrel. Or maybe his father had persuaded Wig he ought to. And there she was again, believing what she wanted to believe.

"You still haven't told me where you went last Sunday," Mrs. Sperrow reminded her daughter.

"Out to the country to paint."

"Oh," her mother said flatly, "you and your paints." She walked around the room, straightening ash trays, fluffing cushions, rearranging violets and lilies-of-the-valley in a bowl. A sudden whiff of the lily fragrance drifted toward Zenty and reminded her of the leaf-soggy patch behind the old house.

"Last week I was upset, Mom."

Mrs. Sperrow glanced up quickly and said in alarm, "Did you and Wig have a fuss?"

"No."

"Well," she said in relief. "I hope you've got some sense. Men are funny, Zenty. You sort of have to read them with a fine tooth comb. When they're grumpy, you just don't pay them any mind." She stopped then as if suddenly aware that her daughter might not consider Mother the best authority on how to get along with men. "Take a man like your father, of course," she said, "and nothing you do is any good." She sniffed a lily-of-the-valley and then placed it in the bowl. "What upset you?"

"Oh, to begin with, I went to a party at the Teilers."

"You *did?* And you're only telling me now? How is the old gentleman?"

Her mother's tone of condescension suddenly tickled Zenty. Mom might stand in awe of the Teiler wealth but not of the Teilers. She could always match them in vitality, and the ability simply to do whatever had to be done— with competence. If she felt any sense of inferiority, it was because her bank account was inferior to theirs.

1 9 5

"My, he must have been surprised," Mother said musingly. "Not to see a little kid for years and years and then suddenly she's a young lady. Rocks you back on your toes, I can tell you." Mom sat down, smiling with pleasure at Mr. Teiler's imagined amazement. "What did he say?" she asked eagerly.

For a moment, Zenty was tempted to lie, but finally said, "He didn't remember me—or pretended not to."

Mrs. Sperrow frowned as if not quite believing. "Why, that's silly," she said, "with Wig crazy about you and all, the old gentleman must know."

"Oh, Mother!" Zenty tried to curb her impatience. "Look, will you tell me something honestly? Are you expecting Wig to marry me?"

Mrs. Sperrow picked up an ash tray of blue bubbled glass and held it to the light. "Funnier things have happened," she said and set the ash tray down again.

"And the money Father sends you're saving for my wedding?"

Mrs. Sperrow flashed around angrily. "And where do you think the money's coming from if I don't? You and your father between you haven't a lick of sense about money. Who's to pay for a fancy wedding I'd like to know?"

"How can you be so sure I'll need one—or even want one?"

"I know you. You and your father both. You act as if the common horde's not good enough for you. Everything for you two has to be special—never mind how, just so's it's different from everybody else's. Look what he used to put in his coffee. Maybe you don't remember. But *chocolate ice cream!* I ask you."

Zenty burst into laughter.

"There," her mother said, pointing at her daughter. "That's exactly what I mean. You *would* think it's funny when all I can see it's just a way to be snubbeley."

"No," Zenty protested, still giggling. "I'm just laughing because partly you're right. But look, Mother," she said, earnestly now, "if you chose to drink molasses in your coffee, Father and I wouldn't care."

"Oh, I know you wouldn't," Mrs. Sperrow declared with vehemence. "Don't I know? Like as not, you wouldn't even notice, much less care."

Again she was right enough to make Zenty uneasy. She got up and walked to the window. On the other side of the hedge that divided the Kohlmans' yard from the neighbor's came scraping noises as of someone emptying flower pots of plants to be set out in the garden. Beside the hedge, two robins rooted in the upturned earth. Suddenly. as so often happened, she was depressed.

"I know your tony ideas," Mom said.

"I have no *tony* ideas about weddings."

"About boy friends you have. I worry that you'll marry somebody like your father—all brains he doesn't know what to do with. That's why—sure I'm hoping you'll marry Wig since you like him and he likes you, and I know you'll be taken care of."

A grackle fluttered down and drove away the robins. Zenty turned back to the room. "Mom, I wish you wouldn't set your heart on my marrying Wig. In the first place, Mr. Teiler does not approve. I know because he told me so."

"What did he tell you?" Mother sounded anxious, and Zenty regretted now that she had started the discussion. Why had she anyway? To jolt Mom or to elicit reassurances that Zenty had misunderstood Mr. Teiler?

"I can't quote verbatim, Mom. Mostly he hinted."

"Oh, well, *hinted*," Mrs. Sperrow said, brightening. "You know you always got a chit on your shoulder, honey. Honestly."

"All the same he offered to get me a job as an airline hostess. Oh, and something else I just remembered," Zenty said, her face tightening with delayed anger. She stared at her mother with narrowed eyes. "He referred to the high marriage rate among airline stewardesses, as if he thought *that* would entice me. He must imagine I'm just out to marry. *Period*."

"Now, now. He's an old man, Zenty, and I don't like you saying things about somebody older like that, and I will say for your father, he wouldn't hear to it either."

Zenty brooded a moment. "Oh, well, I suppose if you're objective," she said, "you can't blame Mr. Teiler too much. Nowadays a wife has to be almost as well educated as her husband if she's to help him advance in business."

"I thought Wig was to teach."

"He is. But do you know anything about college campuses, Mother? They're *swarming* with Ph.D.'s."

Suddenly Mrs. Sperrow's face tightened. "So that's what you've been working up to all along," she said. "You made all this up just to—"

"Mother! When did I ever tell you a lie?"

"Ho. Ho," Mother said. "You were always making things up when you were little—telling everybody your father was a duke and lived in England because he had to stay near the Queen. And you even said once that I wasn't your real mother—that you had lots of brothers and sisters and I'd stole you because I didn't have a little girl of my own."

Zenty smiled, but she shifted uncomfortably. "All children have great imaginations," she protested. "I didn't mean anything." Her depression, she thought, was sheer frustration with herself and her inability to accept *any* place as the place she belonged. She sat chewing the inside of her lip and pinching the fingers of her left hand as if to punish herself.

Mother said with glum reflectiveness, "I don't understand the old gentleman. Why, you're just about the prettiest girl in Mt. St. Clare—or almost. And you're smart even if you don't use good sense." She lifted a lock of Zenty's hair and curled it around her finger. "Anyway there are the Sniders who own the market on Front Street. Their boy was in eighth grade with you. Remember?"

Zenty shrugged, and Mom said, "I saw him one day and he was asking about you, and I—" She stopped and bit her lips, and Zenty realized with dismay that her mother had been boasting about Wig. "Oh, well, that's water under the dam. What do you say I invite the Sniders to tea next Sunday?"

Zenty laughed in exasperation. "Will you tell me, please, *why* you're so anxious to marry me off?"

"Now that's a stupid question, Zenty. I want you to be happy." She paused and then said, "All right. I know what you're thinking. But you get a good sensible man who'll bring home a good paycheck every week and—"

"Doesn't love count for anything?" Zenty asked.

"Ye-es," Mother admitted, "but you can get fooled by love, too. Seems to me you can learn to love a steady man if you put your mind to it. I don't just mean you. I mean any girl can. Believe me, I could if I had it to do over again."

"But you and I are different, Mom."

To Zenty's utter astonishment then, Mother turned on her daughter with a blazing anger. "We are *not*," she declared. "We're exactly alike. That's our trouble. That's why we're always scrabbling."

Zenty started to protest, then realized that to do so would be uncomplimentary. "We hardly ever enjoy the same things though," she said hesitantly.

"Because—like I said before—you always have to pretend you're different, you and your father both."

"Maybe we're not pretending."

"Fiddlesticks! You're always proving something to yourself. You think it's smart to be different, and I'm hoping you'll get over it once you're married and settled down."

Zenty sat silently watching her mother's squared capable fingers as they slid the copper medallion back and forth on the chain. And it occurred to her that Mother in her own way was proud of her daughter and for that reason insistent on their being alike and for that reason, too, could not bear differences of opinion that upset her notion, which she must have realized nonetheless was more wish than fact. And perhaps . . .

Zenty turned her gaze to the floral pattern of the draperies. Perhaps Mom objected to college not merely because

2 0 1

of the expense, although that would always figure in Mom's calculations, but because she was afraid her daughter would grow away from her altogether.

The realization did not cheer her. She would always resent any effort to limit her world or to recast her in another mold. She could not give up her enthusiasms or even pretend to. But she could show more admiration for everything in which her mother excelled, Zenty supposed. Or try to. And maybe, *maybe* she could stop arguing.

"Oh, well, Mom," Zenty said, "we're not the only mother and daughter who disagree now and then."

Mother pressed the medallion against her chin. "Woods are full of them," she said, "though I can't say as that excuses you, Zenty." After a pause, she added, "All right, *us.*" She was not one to sit still long, and letting the necklace fall back against her dress, she stood up and arched her back. Then surprisingly she said, "Maybe you ought to read to Hory for a little while."

Zenty considered so as not to appear eager. "Just as you say, Mother. You know what's best for him. I don't. About fifteen minutes, maybe?"

"About fifteen minutes shouldn't hurt," Mother agreed. "And how would it be if I fixed us some hot chocolate and brought it up to his room?"

"Great."

"All right, then." She started for the kitchen. In the

doorway, she stopped. "And, honey," she said, "don't you worry about anything. I've been thinking." She reflected a moment and seemed about to change her mind, but then she said resolutely, "If you should get the promise of a loan for, you know, school . . . If you should—though, mind, I can't for the life of me see where you'll get one—but if you do, why I'll—I'll sign the note."

"Note! Would you have to?" Zenty asked in alarm.

"Somebody would. You're not twenty-one. You might even need a co-signer, but I could fix that up, too."

"Oh!" The word made a small dismal sound in the quiet room. It had never occurred to Zenty that to borrow money might be a complicated affair, involving her parents.

"Well, let's not cross all our bridges at once," Mother said. "And anyway, maybe by next fall you'll be so interested in some nice young man you won't be wanting to go anywhere." She blinked cheerily at her daughter and left for the kitchen.

Zenty walked out into the hall. At the foot of the stairway, she stopped and rested her cheek against her hand on the newel post.

"What a funny world," she murmured and went on up to Hory.

FIFTEEN

With the approaching end of the college year in late May, Zenty was too busy for any further self-reproaches. Wig had announced early in the semester that he would require two term papers, one a biographical and the other a historical essay. With that advance warning, he had told his students, no one needed to be caught in a last-minute flurry. All the same, the class *was* in a last-minute flurry with sighs and cries and groans.

Zenty moaned with the rest, but only to prove to herself that she was a normal student. Actually she enjoyed the research. Each early morning found her in the library— lost in the past and in her dreams of the future, too, for nowhere did she feel so much a student as in the quiet of the library. For her term papers, she had chosen the life of Pepys and the Great Fire of London, 1666. When she told Wig of her choice—standing alone by his desk after class—his eyes began to smile as he recognized that, of course, she could use the same books for research on both subjects. He threw her a knowing sidelong glance.

"You wouldn't by any chance be making life easy for yourself, would you?" he asked.

She giggled. "No, professor. I'm just coordinating my work."

He regarded her for some moments then and said, "Zenty, how on earth am I ever to teach class without you in the front row?"

She colored slightly and said, "Believe me, I'm going to miss the front row."

Another student approached Wig then, and reluctantly Zenty left for the library until time for the clinic to open. In the classroom doorway, she turned to look at him, and to her surprise he was watching her, and now he raised his hand in a half salute. She could not help wondering whether there had been an echo of finality in his words.

She had still in those weeks a sense of unease that had started with the fire at Gyps's school. Since then Aunt Doris had taken on the management of the Blue Gull Gift Shop and more often than not returned home at night weary and late and inclined to be sarcastic. Aunt Rhoda surprised everyone by stepping out one evening (to use her own words) with a widower—a nurseryman and Sunday artist from near Green Meadows. A card arrived from Arnold Sperrow. He was moving back to Spain again. He had had a good year which might or might not mean financially good. Oh, yes, and he still missed his poppet. And everything added up to a restlessness that seeped through the vivid shapes of history with which she lived in those days and the aura of hope for the future.

Just before the closing date of the contest, Zenty managed the extravagance of a taxi to transport her picture to the art gallery. She had signed the painting *Cass Uhlman,* and all the way over, she was scared. She crossed her fingers and murmured, "Please, please, please," meaning, "Please don't let me run into Wig or Mr. Teiler or Gyps or anyone I know—and please, please, let me win."

A woman at the door took the painting from Zenty, gave her a receipt, and a gratuitous wish for good luck. And then almost immediately Zenty began to worry— not about her chances to win, but about Wig and his reactions. She could always explain, of course, that Cass Uhlman was her artist-name, though Wig might well wonder why she had chosen such an unfeminine pseudonym. What troubled her was that he might remember his father's telling her of a wish for a companion picture to *The Red Barn.*

What troubled her really was Cuss Sperrow. She hated suspense at any time, but now the ten days of waiting for the winners announcement stretched an impossible length ahead. Sleep became troubled with dreams though she recalled only snatches of them in the mornings. One vivid remembrance she had of a man who was Wig writing the word *rationalize* on the blackboard. But when he finished and turned around, the man was her father, and he pointed at her and shouted, "Out!" Often she awoke with a sense of doom like an icy finger on her heart.

Watching Wig in class—his relaxed manner, his masculine mannerisms that always enchanted her, the shifts of expression on his face—she became more and more apprehensive. And then often her mind wandered. One morning as she stared out at the magnolias, already shedding browned petals to lie in heaps where the robins hopped about in search of food, Wig called on her. She roused with a start, stammered a moment, and then said, "I'm afraid I didn't hear the question."

"I know you didn't," Wig said. At his slow grin, the class laughed. She smiled, a bit sheepishly, and Wig said, "Will someone please enlighten Miss Sperrow?"

The boy across the aisle obliged, and Zenty then answered so competently that Wig's eyebrows lifted in acknowledgment, and again the class laughed. There could be no doubt that Zenty Sperrow delighted the professor— at times anyway. But was he in love with her? The fact was, of course, that she wanted Wig and college, too, and there was in her mind a fear that she might win the contest and lose him. But then she wondered whether once away at school, she would really miss him all *that* much. Not knowing for certain added to her uneasiness. Even her dreams seemed fuzzy.

On the Saturday before the announcement date, Wig invited her to lunch. They drove out to the Flaming Bush Club and dined on the porch overlooking the golf course that smelled of newly mown grass. A stream cut through the greens at the left and sparkled with May sunshine. Now and then the shadow of a passing cloud darkened the water. Suddenly a golf ball zoomed low, dropped, and sent up a spray. Through the gently stirring air sounded a cry of dismay.

"Tough," Wig commented, and then he and Zenty both sat straighter as the players sauntered into view beyond the porch. Even at this distance, Zenty recognized them —Derek, blond and only slightly taller than the brunette Jocelyn . . . Archer, long-legged and compelled to shorten his natural stride . . . and Nonie with her sunny hair escaping from under a straw hat. She pulled it off and stretched herself full length on her stomach near the water's edge and scanned the stream. Archer lowered himself beside her and with a mashie fished in the brook for the lost golf ball.

Zenty stole a glance at Wig. He had set down his fork

and was watching with a smile of affection. Nonie raised on her elbows and shrugged her shoulders at Archer, but for a moment neither seemed inclined to move. Then Archer rose, dusted off his slacks, and leaning over lifted Nonie. As on the day of the party, she came up limply, sagged against his shoulder, and then laughed at him.

"So that crisis is over," Wig said and began to eat again.

Zenty frowned at her plate. For her, too, in a way the crisis ought to have been over; yet she felt no elation. She said, not meeting his eyes, "Your father will be disappointed."

"Why?" Wig demanded, so aggressively that she flushed.

"He rather fancied Nonie for a daughter-in-law, didn't he?"

Wig went on buttering a piece of roll without replying at first. Then he said, "Oh, I don't know. Father rather likes the *status quo*."

So it was his father who was satisfied with everything just as it was. She wondered. She really did wonder, but then only briefly, for the other crisis troubled her again. Almost she wished she had not heard of the Teiler contest. She picked at the stuffing in the veal birds on her plate. Wig was about to signal the waiter to bring her whatever else she might like when Zenty confessed that she simply was not hungry. Let Wig believe that the excitement of being with him had inhibited her appetite. He would be only partly right. She was far more nervous about what he would think if she won the contest. Would he condone her bit of indirection?

Indirection! That was a good word. Oh, yes, and she could quite hear her father saying, "And where did you fish up that one?"

Forget Father. Forget everybody.

She nibbled again at the veal birds but finally gave up and asked only for coffee when the waiter came for the dessert order.

Shortly after, as she and Wig were leaving the club house, she noted again the painting of the gulls over the mantel in the lounge. She inquired for the artist.

"Guess," Wig said.

"I haven't a notion," she told him.

"Gyps," Wig said.

"I didn't know he was *that* good," she whispered.

"Tops," Wig said. "Look, I thought we might stop off at the art gallery on the way back and sneak a preview of the contest winners. Okay?"

She nodded as she tried to control a sudden chill of excitement.

"Let's see if Gyps is in the shop. Maybe he can get away for an hour."

Gyps was in the shop, leaning against the counter and

throwing a practice golf ball in the air as he talked with two girls and a young man with sideburns. Zenty did not recognize Eddie at first and when she did, her inclination was to walk out of the shop, but, of course, she could not. Gyps saw her then, and his dark eyes brightened. Unconsciously she sighed. Pretty girls Gyps might admire but the one who outmaneuvered him in a contest . . . would he ever forgive? But how could she be sure she had won? And if she had not, at least relief would be the balm to her disappointment. Were there people in this world, she wondered, whose emotions were simple? Who were never torn between wanting and not wanting? What had come over her this past week? The answer followed the question like a root pulled up with a plant. Guilt. Immediately she rejected it, and would have started in on a train of argument with herself had not Gyps sauntered over with Eddie behind him.

"Hi, ya," Gyps said and held out the practice ball to Zenty. It was hollow and full of small holes for lightness. "Field mice," he told her with a solemn face. "Frightful this year. Look what they've done to our best golf balls."

"Artistic mice," she commented and drew closer to Wig as Eddie observed her from tip to toe.

"The only kind Gyps will tolerate," Wig said. "Look, you joker, Zenty and I are headed for the gallery. Want to come along and take a squint at the winners?"

Gyps hesitated and then said, sorry, but he could not leave the shop and he doubted anyway that there would be anything specially exciting in the contest. But his elaborate indifference did not fool Zenty, and she was sure now that he awaited the outcome as anxiously as she. Wig turned to chat with Eddie for a few seconds—about golf scores and handicaps—while Zenty questioned Gyps on his plans for fall and learned that he had none . . . yet.

She was about to depart with Wig when Gyps said, "Oh, hey, I've got something to show you." He pulled out his wallet and sorted through papers—dog-eared letters, torn scraps of a drawing pad, driver's license, car registration, social security card.

"Oh, heck," he said, "must have left it in my other suit —euphemistically known as my *good* suit." He started to stuff the papers back into the wallet, then exclaimed, "No, here it is." And he drew out a crumpled blue-gray folder, replaced his wallet, and smoothed out the leaflet.

"For me or Wig?" Zenty asked.

"For you. One of the brochures your father sent out to advertise his school. Never know what you'll find when you start scrounging around for a stamp. Never know what *I'll* find, that is. Hey, Wig, look here." Gyps held up the folder for them to see the reproduction of a painting on the front. "Doesn't this remind you of your father's *Red Barn?*"

Wig frowned and said, "Yes, rather," with the sort of impatience he usually showed at mention of Arnold Sperrow or his work. But Zenty scarcely heard, for her heart had contracted tightly. The brochure! Of course. *It* was the reason for the many barn scenes Father had painted. But why had he *had* to pick the very one *she* had chosen to adapt for the contest? Because the painting was the best of the lot obviously. No mystery there—only incredibly bad luck. What in the world was she to do now? Eddie had come up behind her and was scanning the brochure over her shoulder. And in her frustration she would gladly have used him as her whipping boy for all her anger at herself, would happily have stamped on his toes. So she felt briefly, then thought, poor Eddie, he might be a jerk, but he was not to blame that Zenty Sperrow was a stupid fool.

Gyps spoke, "What's the matter, kid? Ghosts?"

"Sort of," she said. In a swift possessive gesture, Wig turned her toward the door. "We'd better shove off," he said, and to Gyps, "Sorry you can't come with us. See you, boy."

He and Eddie followed them onto the shop stoop and waved after them. But she was too worried now to focus

her thoughts on anyone. Would Wig . . . would Gyps
. . . would Eddie recognize her painting as a copy—adaptation of the barn scene on the brochure? Oh, *copy, adaptation.* What difference did words make? She had been rash, and now almost certainly would lose Gyps as a friend. And Wig? Her fingertips prickled. She felt as if she had been sitting on her hands. Her head had begun to ache dully. She ought to ask Wig to take her home. Should she? And wait and worry all weekend and be afraid even to look at the Monday papers—not to mention facing Wig in class. What a coward she was.

Wig talked as they rode along, and now and then she said, "Yes," or, "No," until they neared the museum, and he reached over and clasped her hand.

"What's the matter, Zenty?" he asked, "You haven't behaved like yourself all week. You know that?"

"End-of-term jitters," she said.

"*You?* Come off it!"

She debated then whether to confess to Wig, but if her painting had not won, and he did not recognize Cass Uhlman as Cassandra Uhlman Sarah Sperrow, then he need never know her—her maneuver. Oh, all right, deceit. Call it by its proper name. She began to pray she had not won.

Wig parked behind the museum, and they walked along beside a wall where wisteria reached out tendrils. One brushed her arm with a ghostly touch, and she started violently, then controlled herself. And now she felt needled to hurry, hurry. End the suspense. She was so close to knowing now that she could not bear another moment of heart pounding and prickling hands.

Wig paused to talk to an attendant while she stood clasping and unclasping her purse. Realizing then how she betrayed her nervousness, she stopped and reminded herself to relax. Shoulders, relax. Arms, relax. Hands, relax. Fingers, relax. And in a minute, I'll fall apart, she told herself. Wig motioned to her, and they rode the elevator to the third floor. And there was more delay as another attendant led them to the rear of the building, unlocked a door, and signaled them to wait. As if the walls were covered with Rembrandts, she thought. As if there were a meeting going on of the Secret Society of International Spies. Let's stick our heads in the doorway and yell, "Boo!"

She began to count silently to mesmerize away her fears.

The attendant returned and said, "All right, sir." And Wig and Zenty stepped into a long room where tea service was being set up for the morrow. At the far end of the gallery, Mr. Teiler stood in conference with a tall, lanky man and a slight woman—both of whom Zenty recognized from newspaper pictures as the other two judges and who, according to the art store gossip, had been picked more for their amenability to suggestion than for their knowledge of art.

Zenty caught the scene fleetingly in mind, only enough for awareness, and at once glanced swiftly about seeking the ribbons that proclaimed the winners. And there on the opposite wall . . . Her heart flipped over with such suddenness that she held her breath. There *Barn in Springtime* sported a blue ribbon. But which prize? Which *prize?*

Wig took her arm. "Here's Gyps's," he said, and turned her toward the nearer wall and a white-beribboned painting. It was simple—so simple both in concept and execution as to be deceptive. A winter scene with a fence and open gate; a rectangle of light, presumably from a window, falling across footprints in snow; a corner of a porch on one side; a branch of fir tree on the other; shadows; and that was all. She could only applaud the cleverness with which Gyps had contrived his painting. There was an economy of line to delight the impressionist, a medley and balance of shapes with emphasis on the square and rectangular to please the abstractionist, and enough of the pictorial with emotional overtones to satisfy the classicist.

She had almost forgotten her own involvement, almost forgotten Wig's presence until he moved closer to the painting and read, *"December Dusk.* Second Prize. Oh, wouldn't you know?" he muttered and then in a tone of disgust, "Let's see who won first."

She did not follow but watched as he walked up to her

painting, backed away, and scowling thrust his hands in his pockets. Well, now he knew. Only surely he could not imagine that all these weeks she had been using him to learn his father's artistic likes and dislikes so as to plan her little strategy. Wig understood that she did not exploit friendships. Or did he?

Mr. Teiler hurried over to his son and clapped him on the shoulder. "Amazing, isn't it?" he said in a hearty voice. "The likeness, I mean." Wig continued to scowl, and his father said, "Oh, naturally, there's not the intrinsic quality of *The Red Barn*. But for a young amateur to paint with such faithfulness is most gratifying. By the way, do you know this Cass Uhlman?"

Wig shrugged faintly, and his father said, "Oh, I understand, Wig. You wanted your young friend, what's-his-name, to win, and I'm sorry I couldn't oblige you, but I *had* to be objective. You know that."

"Objective!" Wig said scornfully. "Oh, Father, take your tongue out of your cheek. This Cass Uhlman knew precisely what to paint to please you, and you've fallen right into the trap."

"Now, now, wait a minute. Wa-ait a minute, boy. I've been around too long to fall into traps. Traps!" he repeated disgustedly. "This painting has a freshness and a charm that show definite promise in a young artist."

"Oh, freshness, charm, Father! For heaven's sake! A

poster may have freshness and charm. What does this picture say that your *Red Barn* hasn't already said? And look at the brush work. It's obviously an imitation."

"Well, now, wait a minute, Wig. I don't like that word, 'imitation.' One reason for my choice . . ." He did not, Zenty noticed, even pretend to include the other judges. ". . . is that I hope to encourage the young artist to learn from his betters."

Wig shook his head at his father, and Mr. Teiler patted his son on the shoulder. "Wig, I know. I know you're disappointed that what's-his-name?—Di Costa?—didn't win."

"Father, he *deserved* to win. That's the point I'm making." Wig stretched his arm toward the opposite wall. "Look at what he has achieved. Without depicting a solitary human figure or even that of an animal, he has created vividly a sense of life and yet a marvelous serenity. I could live with that picture and find it fresh twenty years from now. And you talk about freshness."

Mr. Teiler pinched his lower lip thoughtfully. "The minute I saw *this* painting," he said, nodding at *Barn in Springtime,* "I knew I had a winner—my hunch was that strong."

"Oh, *Father,*" Wig said with a laugh. "You don't judge a contest on hunches."

"Well, *no,* not without critical judgment, too. But don't

forget, my hunches haven't failed me over a good many years, son."

"Well, okay. Let's hope the critics have the same hunches. Have you forgotten the critics, Father? They'll be here from all over—from the *Tribune,* the *Times,* from *Artists and Collectors,* maybe *Life.*"

"I certainly hope so," Mr. Teiler said vehemently. "I hope, what's more, that in some modest way our selection will help restore old and lost values to the arts." He sounded as if he were rehearsing a planned speech to reporters.

"By lost values, you mean precise draftsmanship, I suppose," Wig said dryly.

"That, yes. Most certainly that."

Wig sighed loudly. "Father, I'm not convinced you haven't been tricked. You have awarded first prize to an *imitation* of one of your favorite pictures—and a deliberate imitation, I'll wager."

"What are you saying? That this chap read the article in *Artists and Collectors?*"

Wig shrugged. "Something like that."

Zenty waited no longer. She tiptoed quickly to the door and once out in the corridor, she ran, and the click-click of her heels resounded all about her. She fled down the two flights of stairs with the staccato sounds echoing in her ears, hurried past the guard and out into the spring sunshine. She paused a moment, blinking against the sudden glare, and strained for the sound of Wig's voice, the pounding of his footsteps behind her. But all she heard were the ordinary city noises—a motor starting up, the slam of a car door, the honk of a horn, a tin can kicked along the gutter. She crossed the street and walked two blocks to a bus stop. There she sat down on a bench in the corner of a shelter and tried to sort out her thoughts.

She had won. That fact she must, must cling to. She had won, and next fall would find her away at school with a whole new world to explore. Now she must begin to plan what she would do about clothes. Maybe she could earn extra money by working overtime in the clinic this summer. June, July, August, part of September. More than three months of . . .

. . . of scorn to face. For make no mistake, she had opened Pandora's box. Wig must already have recognized her painting as a copy of the one on her father's brochure. And soon Gyps would, too. And Eddie. Wouldn't he delight to whisper, "Fraud," all through the artists' group? But the die was cast. She had won. What could she do but accept graciously and hope? She blew her nose softly.

No use to go home and confess to the aunts. Doris's tongue would wither Miss Zenty down until she could stand on a dime with room to spare. And Rhoda could not be counted on for sympathy either. Imagine the buzz-ing in the art store on Monday with poor Rhoda right in the midst of it all. Not to mention Zenty Sperrow in the middle of a great big fat mess just when she ought to be happy and excited about school. She could prepare all summer, but who would rejoice with her?

She paced the length of the bus shelter and back again. A youngster clattering by on the opposite side of the street stopped and gaped at her. She wondered whether she had been talking aloud, gesturing with her hands. She slid back on the bench into a protected corner. Anyone might well imagine she had taken leave of her senses. Well, so she had. Who would write now: "Miss Sperrow's high school grades may have fallen somewhat below standards, but I have found her an alert student, amazingly honest." How often had she imagined Wig writing those words? And now he would not—ever.

But she must not think of Wig now or she would cry. Amazing how a single dishonest act could set off a chain reaction of trouble. She sat biting her thumb. Now a new worry prickled through her other anxieties: If there should be even a hint of scandal, only whispers of fraud, wouldn't the art schools hear, all the same? And what school would welcome a student suspected of trickiness?

"Oh, *grief!*" she exclaimed with feeling. But what could she do? What was there to do now?

She had a vague notion that buses had stopped and started, leaving behind the smell of exhaust, and that at some moment a black Rolls, carrying a chauffeur and a man with a gold-headed cane, had gone by. She heard the grinding of brakes then and impulsively jumped to her feet as a bus halted outside the shelter. She climbed aboard, asked for the stop nearest Magnolia Drive, and having paid her fare, sat tensely in a front seat. Her stomach fluttered, but Cuss Sperrow had got herself into this mess, and it was up to her—and no one else—to get herself out.

She began to chew the inside of her cheek as the bus carried her toward the Teiler home.

SIXTEEN

Several times as she walked the interminable length from the Teiler gateway to the house with its rows of watchful windows, she hesitated, needled to turn back. But she went on, resisting the path through the herb garden and the woods beyond that would take her to the street without risk of meeting Wig on his return. All the way toward the house, she prayed that she would not make a fool of herself. Butterflies in her stomach or no, she had to *appear* calm.

In the shelter of the veranda, as she listened to the echo of the doorbell chimes, she began to rehearse what she would say to Mr. Teiler. A maid let Zenty in and at first refused to announce her. But Zenty insisted.

"He'll *want* to see me. Cass Uhlman—tell him—about the art contest. It's urgent."

The next moments of waiting were frustrating. She had not questioned for an instant that Mr. Teiler would at least listen to her or that she would retrieve *Barn in Springtime*. To divert her mind, she busied herself with little things—pushed back a lock of hair, removed her gloves and tucked them into her purse, pulled out a tissue and wiped her palms. Constantly she reminded herself that any show of nervousness would annoy Mr. Teiler. Finally the maid returned and asked Zenty to step into the study.

Mr. Teiler sat behind his desk with a disgruntled expression on his large-featured face. The cigar in his hand had smoldered until a long length of ash clung to the end. The air smelled of cigar smoke. She wondered whether he was out of sorts with himself or Wig or her for intruding.

He rose and nodded to her. He did not appear surprised that Cass Uhlman was Zenty Sperrow. But then perhaps he had long since disciplined himself against surprises. He indicated a leather chair, and as she perched on the edge of it, he sat down again behind his desk. At first neither spoke.

Then she said, "Mr. Teiler, I would like to withdraw my picture from the contest."

His eyebrows shot up in a manner reminiscent of Wig. She started to bite her lip and then stopped and reminded herself again that she simply must appear relaxed and confident.

"At this late date, Miss Sperrow?" he inquired. "You are Cass Uhlman, I take it."

She explained the Cassandra and Uhlman in her name.

"Your professional name—Cass Uhlman?"

"Not exactly. *Cass* sounds like a boy, and I thought a boy might have a better chance of winning than a girl."

Mr. Teiler covered his mouth with his left hand and pinched his nose between thumb and forefinger as with his right hand he knocked the ash from his cigar.

"You're throwing a monkey wrench into the works. You know that, don't you? Or do you? I'll have to phone the other judges. My secretary will have to rewrite the releases for tomorrow. Pictures will have to be rearranged. A nuisance all the way round."

"I am sorry, but—"

"Why do you want to withdraw? Because of Wig? And what he said about your painting, eh?"

"Well, no—not exactly. You see, I cheated, and if I were discovered, you'd be as embarrassed as I."

"Cheated!" he exclaimed, scowling at her. "How? How do you cheat in an art contest?"

She told him. And he went on scowling, and his cigar went on smoldering as he listened. At length, he said, "Did Wig put you up to this?"

She glared at him. "No, certainly not," she said. She remembered her vow to stay at least outwardly calm, and folding her hands in her lap, relaxed a little. "No, sir," she said.

He regarded her critically the way a child does. "How did you know I wanted another barn picture?"

"You *told* me," she said, "the day of Wig's party."

"*I* did?"

"When I was looking at my father's picture."

"Eh?"

"*The Red Barn.*"

He cocked an eye at the end of his cigar as he rolled it in the ash tray on his desk, then glanced back at her with an odd smile.

"It *is* his picture," she said. "It's signed with his outline of a sparrow and I can show you where."

He jerked forward in his chair, swiveled around, and propelled it to a book shelf behind him. He swung back to his desk with the March copy of *Artists and Collectors,* flipped open the magazine to the center spread, and beckoned her with a waggle of his hand. She walked over and stood beside him.

"Now where's this bird you're talking about?" he demanded.

She pointed to the clump of leaves and explained that the sparrow was barely discernible, if at all, on the reproduction. She delineated a bird with her fingertip and then discovered that Mr. Teiler was watching not her hand but her face. Disconcerted, she kept her head averted but she was aware that he still contemplated her. Then he opened his desk drawer, drew out a magnifying glass, and studied the leaves.

"Not very distinct. I suppose you checked it on the original."

"Yes, sir."

He stared at her again speculatively, and it occurred to her that he was not deliberately trying to make her uncomfortable. He was—as her father used to say—rearranging his thoughts.

"Hmmmm," Mr. Teiler said at last. "And the contest painting, I take it, is your father's, too? That might account for my hunch."

"Oh, well, no," she said.

"Then I don't see."

"Barn in Springtime," she explained, "is a *copy* of one of my father's paintings—the one he used on his brochure for his art school."

"Well, now," Mr. Teiler said, "let's stay out of the art school, eh? Things are complicated enough, eh? What I want to know is—did *you*," pointing the stub of his cigar at her, "copy the painting?"

"Yes, sir. I painted the picture," she said, "but I did not

create it. Of course, it does take skill to copy a picture faithfully, but you don't copy the *Mona Lisa,* say, and stick a couple of cows in the background and claim the picture as your own." She spoke indignantly as if lecturing him instead of herself. He cupped his hand over his mouth and rubbed his fingers along his nose.

"And besides," she said, "if your contest had called for *just* barn paintings as suitable companion pieces for *The Red Barn* and everybody had submitted barn scenes, then maybe I should not have been quite so unfair. But I did take advantage, and that is partly what I meant when I said I had cheated."

His hand still covered his mouth, and the obvious effort to hide his amusement angered her. She was not a silly child full of histrionics. She did not enjoy her own drama so much that she would give up a dream in the process, for pete's sake. She blew her nose softly and Mr. Teiler said, "Hmmmm." He gazed around his study walls at framed pen-and-ink drawings of various objects, possibly sketched by him for agency purposes. There were groupings of silver flatware, including sugar tongs, a series of piston rings, an electric can opener, a fist holding a monkey wrench—all exquisitely drawn. Zenty could not remember seeing more detailed draftsmanship. And yet all were as stiff and lifeless and unexciting as a hunk of lead pipe.

"You youngsters!" he said, suddenly, explosively. "You have talent, and what do you do with it? Putter around in a dilettantish sort of way. If I were your age and able to paint anything as fresh as your *Barn in Springtime,* do you think I'd be operating a switchboard?" He rubbed one eyebrow with his knuckle. "But then a young girl, I suppose, has her reasons."

She bit her thumb hard as she battled threatening tears. To be accused of indifference on top of everything else that had happened seemed to her miserably unjust. She sat struggling with herself, afraid that if she spoke, she would cry. Mr. Teiler straightened his desk calendar, nudged a polished black stone, settled his pen firmly in its holder.

"Very well, Miss Cassandra," he said, surprising her momentarily with the use of her first name. "You've upset the applecart, but I've picked up apples and carts before this." He nodded, smiling at her, and she was dismissed.

But still she lingered, for now was the moment to tell him how desperately she wanted to go away to school and to ask if he could help her borrow money. Almost at once she knew she could not. She was afraid of what he and Wig might conjecture—afraid they might imagine that all along she had deliberately maneuvered her friendship with Wig to her own advantage. And then she wondered whether even such thoughts were not an excuse for delay because she was too proud to discuss money.

In any case, the brief moment of opportunity vanished as Mr. Teiler flipped a button on the intercom box on his desk, and a masculine voice said, "Yes, Mr. Teiler."

"Hold up the contest releases until I talk with you."

A pause and then, "Yes, sir," the voice replied.

"A couple of changes," Mr. Teiler said. He did not sound vexed, and it occurred to Zenty that he might possibly feel relieved to rectify his mistaken choice, might recognize that she had got him off the hook. Certainly now the critics would applaud the award to Gyps.

She said good-bye and went out into the hall. In a moment, she would realize how bereft she was of her dreams and she tried to keep herself from thinking for just a little longer. A bowl of lilacs stood on the hall table, and their fragrance surrounded her suddenly with the hurtful gaiety of spring. She let herself out through the front door and raced swiftly down the steps as if to propel herself forward to next week or the week after, by which time she would have digested her disappointments—would have substituted new dreams for old.

She started to run down the walk when she saw Wig. He stood resting against his car with his arms folded. Unsmiling, he waited for her. When she stopped beside him, he said, "I could shake you."

She watched a dried magnolia leaf—blown by the breeze —skitter under the car. An end of hair caught in her eyelashes and she untangled it.

"I thought you'd understand," she said.

"What was I supposed to understand?" Wig demanded, "That you'd gone off in search of a powder room? Or gone down to the courtyard to commune with the tulips? Or decided to take a walk? Or what? I waited for you. I searched for you. I worried about you. And on second thought, I could spank you."

The magnolia leaf danced a whirling jig and settled against the front tire.

"Well." She sighed in discouragement. "Don't you see? I had to get away by myself and think things over. And anyway, everything's all right now. At least all right for Gyps. I've taken my picture out of the exhibit."

"*Zenty!*" He tapped her on the arm. "Am I supposed to know what you're talking about?"

"*Yes.*"

"Well, I don't."

The breeze whisked a handful of petals along the drive as she stared past the car in perplexity. "You mean you hadn't guessed?" she asked. "I was *sure* you had guessed."

"Guessed what, Zenty? Are we playing games?"

"Cass Uhlman," she said spiritedly. "Cassandra Uhlman."

He rubbed his knuckles over his chin, and his eyebrows pulled sharply together above his blue eyes. Suddenly his face cleared. "Ohhh," he said, "Winner of the first prize. *You?*"

"*Yes,*" she said, her voice deliberately low. "*Me.*"

He began to laugh. And she said heatedly, "But I was sure you suspected . . . especially when your father asked you about Cass Uhlman and you didn't answer. Why didn't you answer?"

"Probably because I didn't hear the question. Look, Zenty, I wasn't thinking about Cass Uhlman. I was thinking about Gyps and my father and worrying that *this* time the critics would make mincemeat of him."

"Oh. I suppose." She still did not want to believe.

Abruptly he chuckled again. Then shaking his head, he said, "I've never known a girl more full of surprises." He put an arm around her as he opened the car door. "Climb in." He settled behind the wheel, stretched his legs sideways, and smiled at her. "All right. Now tell Uncle Wig *allll* about it."

She did not wish to relate the whole story over again— to *Uncle* Wig or anyone else. Not only did she yearn to forget as quickly as possible, but she had an uncomfortable notion that she was about to make unwelcome discoveries. And she was moreover in no mood to tolerate his air of indulgence. He was certainly not very observant if he had not noticed the similarity between her painting and the reproduction on the brochure. How could he not have? she thought incredulously, and instantly answered her own question. A three-by-five that he had scarcely glanced at? Maybe, after all, it did not much resemble the sizable blue-ribboned picture on the gallery wall.

Wig nudged her with his elbow. "Hey, remember me?"

She nodded. "Only I don't know where to start."

But shortly she did, flicking the handle of her purse and occasionally glancing at him as his expression shifted and changed. She finished with a sigh that seemed to rise from a hollowness inside her.

"You mean to say," Wig inquired, "that you've known all along about your father's signature on our painting?"

"Only since the party."

"And you never told us? Why?"

She rested her chin on her purse handle. "You didn't *want* to know," she murmured.

"Now that's a stupid remark," Wig said sharply, but the swift rise of his anger betrayed him.

"Not really you didn't," she insisted. "You were so sure I was bragging."

He shifted his feet. Sunshine, filtering in from the side window, highlighted the polish of his shoes.

"Aren't you being Cuss Sperrow?"

Was she? "Maybe," she admitted—unnecessarily critical

of him perhaps. Nobody relished being proved wrong nor having his images upset.

"Well, stop," he said, and after a moment remarked, "So you cheated and now you've uncheated."

She nodded.

"You've got courage, kid," he observed.

"Frankly," she admitted, "I was too scared to worry about whether I had or hadn't."

"Why?" he asked.

"Why what? Why was I scared? Don't you understand?"

"No."

"Look," she said excitedly. "I was in trouble."

"Why?"

"Oh, Wig, don't keep asking 'why.' I should think it was obvious why. You'd seen the brochure." She gestured northward in the general direction of the golf course. "All right, so you didn't notice the resemblance to my copy. Gyps might have or Eddie. Or the original that my father painted might very well have been sold here in Mt. St. Clare. Let one of the losers in the contest become disgruntled and start nosing around, and there could have been a nice little scandal."

Wig grinned at her, and she said, "You think I'm play-acting, don't you?"

"Nnn-no."

"Well, I'm not," she declared hotly. "Whatever you or anyone else may believe, in my father's code and mine, what I did was cheating."

"Oh, come on now, Cuss," Wig said with exaggerated patience. "Must you always be so supersensitive? All I'm saying is that conscience is a strange, strange thing."

She traced the ridges on the car's leather upholstery. And Wig said, "Look, Zenty, everybody knows you loved the old barn. And everybody knows your father taught you to paint. So what would be more natural than for you to come up with a barn scene that resembled your father's work?"

"You don't think then," she said in astonishment, "that anybody would have ever suspected I'd . . . pulled tricks?"

"Oh, you could never be sure. But the chances were slim." Wig rested his elbow against the back of the seat and his cheek on his palm.

"But *I* knew," she said, "and after seeing Gyps's work—both at the club and at the exhibit—I knew how unfair I had been to Gyps. Especially to him." She watched a moth flutter from the ground and settle on the glossy leaves of the rhododendron. "And all summer," she said, "I'd have gone on rationalizing—gone on arguing with myself, trying to convince myself that the ends justified the means. And underneath, I'd have been scared of discovery." She turned indignantly to Wig. "And now I'm not drama-tizing."

"All right. All right," he said.

"And something else," Zenty said, holding up one finger. Wig grabbed it in his fist.

"Something else?"

She did not reply immediately. Why go on explaining what he already knew—that she hated cheaters and could not much admire herself had she accepted the prize? And, not liking herself, would have suspected that no one else did, would have looked for scorn and taken offense when none was meant.

"The old jelly bean story," she said. But Wig was not so much interested as amused by her earnestness, she de-cided, and sighed softly. They were silent for a while as he traced with his thumb the outline of her fingernail. Unconsciously she sighed again, so deeply that Wig raised his head and regarded her, questioningly.

"You must have wanted to win very badly," he ob-served.

"Yes, I . . . did." She laughed to cover the catch in her voice.

"As much as all that?"

She nodded. "I intended to go to college in the fall if I won."

His eyebrows shot up in surprise. "Oh?" He tapped his

heel softly against the car floor, scowling as if he could not quite make up his mind whether or not he approved.

"Why shouldn't I want to?" she demanded.

"No reason, only . . . I thought I knew you."

Two of them, then, had thought that they had known each other. But did anyone ever, truly?

At length, he said imperatively, "Why didn't you tell me?"

She shrugged and waited, wary but hopeful. Certainly she had learned enough about Wig by now to know that he would not want her to anticipate any ideas he might have for helping her. He asked then whether she had spoken to his father.

"About what?" she inquired cautiously. "A . . . loan?"

"Well, yes, I suppose a loan."

"If . . . if I got help to go away to school," she said, "it would have to be a loan."

"All *right,*" he said and pondered again. Finally he reached across her and opened the car door. "Hop out. We're going in and talk with Father right now."

She hesitated only briefly. Her heart began to pound with excitement as she walked around the back of the car, along the drive, and up the veranda steps. Wig still frowned as he said musingly, "I won't be here in the fall, but I may come back in February to start teaching again if my thesis advisor begins his sabbatical then. That's all beside the point, of course. Monday we'll see about enrolling you at Mt. St. Clare."

She stopped abruptly at the door, and he said, "Now what?" and with a flash of dimples, "Grades?"

She was tempted to say yes, to listen as he explained how he would persuade the dean of admissions to accept Zenty Sperrow. Influential Big Brother Wig! But why should he not be—even consider himself such if he chose? Was she not pigeonholing, too, pinning on labels? She who hated them. For that moment she was tempted to settle even for mediocre training in art, to go on living with the aunts, though maybe a dormitory would prove equally economical and spare them the extra room they needed. And maybe before the last blizzard of the new year, Wig would return. She saw in a hazy flash their joyous reunion in the shelter of the library with snow flying about them.

Wig said, "I may be teaching a sophomore lit course by the time you're ready for one. Who knows?" He flipped his finger at her chin. "Something to look forward to."

She shook away the dream. "For whom? Me?" she asked and bulged her cheek with her tongue.

"Who else?" he said teasingly. *"Zenty!* You know I should enjoy nothing more than to discover my favorite pupil back in the front row."

Yes. Yes, was that not precisely what she did know—
that Wig, like his father, would gladly preserve the *status
quo*. Or so he imagined at the moment anyway. Keep
everything as it was, including his star pupil . . . his occasional Cinderella. But first came summer and then fall
and winter. And who could predict how his plans might
change? But more important than any other considera-
tion: She had that day relinquished a contest so as not to
lose Zenty. She would not lose her now, and if that fantasy reunion-in-a-snow-storm ever happened anywhere, it
would be on a campus of her choice and because Wig
desired to see her—desired strongly enough to go wherever she was.

Oddly she did not feel compelled even to argue . . . to
convince him or herself. She was suddenly eager to talk
with Mr. Teiler again. As she stepped into the hall, a
breeze rustling through from the outdoors stirred the
scent of the lilacs. Wig crossed to the study and knocked.
Simultaneously the grandfather clock by the stairs began
to strike ponderously, reminding Zenty of the clock on
the church across from the clinic. And briefly the world
spread wide, hinting of mystery and of change and of
spring returning ever afresh. But now the prescience was
swift, and though not lingering, prophetic of a happiness
to come.

239

ABOUT THE AUTHOR

Helen Pundt, author of *Spring Comes First to the Willows,* a sensitive story about a young girl, says of her writing: "I always know . . . a great deal more about the characters than appears in the story—both their past and their future. The fun, for me, is learning about them; the hard part is deciding the significant parts of the story; and the hardest, of course, is getting the first draft down on paper."

Miss Pundt, a native of Rochester, New York, received her B.S. degree from Iowa State University at Ames, where she majored in home economics education and minored in journalism. She taught feature writing for a short time at the university.

During the war she worked as an information specialist in Washington, D.C., and later was assistant editor in the extension division at Cornell University's College of Home Economics. More recently, she was senior editor at the General Foods Corporation.

Miss Pundt has traveled throughout Europe and much of the United States, as well as Canada and Mexico. She lives in Yonkers, New York.